CARRIE BEAMER

Evernight Teen ®

www.evernightteen.com

Copyright© 2024

Carrie Beamer

ISBN: 978-0-3695-0981-9

Cover Artist: Jay Aheer

Editor: Melissa Hosack

CARRIE BEAMER

DEDICATION

Experiencing your own love reflected back by another person is one of life's most wonderful blessings.

Thank you Justin Horton for giving me that gift.

You are my Frankie.

CARRIE BEAMER

Some people have to live while others get to sit this living thing out.

—PETER HEDGES, What's Eating Gilbert Grape.

Sometimes the things presented to us as choices aren't choices at all.

—STEPHEN KING, 11/22/63

CARRIE BEAMER

Carrie Beamer

Copyright © 2024

Chapter One

The decision to give my older brother, Jojo, a second chance at life rested heavily on my shoulders as I grappled with the enormity of the power I held. Haunting thoughts of his months spent unable to venture beyond the confines of his bedroom plagued me like nothing ever had before, and the idea of reversing the course of time, transporting him back to a point in his life where he hadn't eaten himself into a prison, terrified me.

The night I discovered I could change the misfortune crushing my brother's very spirit was brought about by Ponyboy, my always under your feet, devious cat. As anyone who has crossed paths with this sly creature knows, he possesses an astonishing knack for weaving himself between our feet at the most inopportune times, causing us to falter and lose our footing, often resulting in spilled drinks or dropped objects.

It's a devious game he seems to relish, and I have no doubt that he takes great pleasure in our misery, cackling like the crazy mastermind he is as we stumble and fall. Little did I know that his evil shenanigans would lead me to discover the miraculous power that would change the course of my life.

As I carefully prepared to take a heaping plate of piping hot spaghetti up to my brother's room, my brain consumed with the task ahead, I was suddenly under attack. A whirl of flying noodles and sauce, courtesy of the cunning tactics of Ponyboy went everywhere. The once semi-clean kitchen was now a chaotic scene of red splattered cabinets and puddles of sauce resembling a murder scene straight out of a horror film. Somehow the dang cat escaped the kitchen without a drop of tomato sauce on his plush fur.

He was good, real good.

Overwhelmed and wanting to strangle Pony, I abandoned my mission to get Jojo his dinner and went outside for some fresh air. As I settled into the well-worn, plastic seat of the dilapidated swing set in my backyard, I was greeted by the creaking of its rusty chains. Even though my shirt was drenched in sauce, the swing set seemed like the ideal spot to find solace from the chaos I'd just left in the kitchen.

The swing set was gifted to me and Jojo by our parents when I was around six or seven years old. We'd barely used it, except for the occasional slide ride, which served as a makeshift ramp to race our Hot Wheel cars down. We preferred to explore the streets surrounding our neighborhood, instead of remaining stuck to the backyard where we felt like we were being watched. In our young minds, swing sets were for babies, and by God we were grown. Looking back, we were too young to be traipsing all over our neighborhood, but that's just what kids did, and we had the time of our lives doing it.

I pumped my legs back and forth, grasping tightly

onto the chilly, metallic chains with both hands. I was surprised how much I loved the sensation of soaring into the moonlit sky. It gave me a sense of freedom to have the crisp, night breeze coursing through my short hair, causing my eyes to water and my nose to drip. The dizzying effect that washed over me every time I propelled myself forward into the open air was exhilarating. How could I have neglected this vessel of joy my whole childhood? A small, involuntary grin crept across my face as I gingerly wiped away the remnants of tomato sauce, dotted across my forehead, with my soggy sleeve.

From my vantage point, I was able to catch a glimpse of my brother engrossed in playing Duck Hunt in his bedroom. The sight of him gnawing on his tongue and maniacally pointing the bright orange, fake gun at the television screen in order to eliminate every airborne duck was alarming to witness. It was clear to me that Nintendo had hit the jackpot with this new ploy to trap boys into the all-consuming realm of video games. What would they think of next?

About my ninth or tenth catapult into the sky, just as my thoughts drifted to the unavoidable cleanup that was waiting for me inside the house, I yearned to return to the minute before the spaghetti storm had erupted in the kitchen.

Suddenly, and without warning, I felt a strange disturbance beneath me. The ground appeared to quiver slightly, causing the sturdy poles of the swing set—that had been stuck in the ground for the past decade—to lift just a bit. With my feet dangling several feet above the grass below, I was unable to see anything unusual happening, but I felt it. The weirdness didn't last long, but I definitely knew something strange was going on. I dragged my sock-clad feet through the overgrown lawn to stop myself as I scanned the yard for any signs of the bizarre shaking. Nothing seemed out of place, and the weird rumble I'd just experienced appeared to have vanished into thin air.

Jumping off the swing, I scurried up the back-patio steps. My body felt like it had been through something odd, but I had no idea how to explain it. It was like when you jump on a trampoline for too long and get off. You feel off balance and somewhat weird, but nothing is wrong with you. Tripping on the loose top step, I stumbled into the screen door. It swung open and delivered me onto the kitchen floor. I almost landed on Ponyboy, whose screeching meow let me know he was appalled at my entrance even though he'd caused this whole disaster in the first place.

My whole body was in a state of panic.

To my surprise, I wasn't sitting in the mess that was there not even ten minutes ago, and the spaghetti was still boiling away in the pot on the stove. My heart slammed into my throat when I looked down and saw that, to my utter amazement, my shirt was entirely spotless. I looked around our cozy kitchen with its olive green, painted cabinets and our sturdy, oak kitchen table that belonged to my grandmother before we inherited it. Everything looked seemingly undisturbed, with no indications of the mayhem that had taken place only moments earlier.

Ponyboy regarded me with an intense and knowing glare, his luminous yellow eyes shining with a hint of mischief, as if he too was aware of the events that had unfolded. He knew something strange was going on.

Cats always know.

As my mom entered the kitchen, the worn floorboards of our old house groaned beneath her weight, announcing her arrival. She stood in the doorway, her long, black hair messily piled atop her head. She helped herself to a piece of the crusty bread I was going to serve with the pasta. She tore off a chunk of the bread's heel with her teeth and adjusted the book she held in her hand. "You look like you've seen a ghost. Why are you on the floor?" She looked down at Ponyboy, figuring he was the culprit.

I silently continued to scan the kitchen in disbelief.

"Dessy? Des?"

She tilted her head sideways, curiously examining me as breadcrumbs littered her shirt.

"Did you make more spaghetti? I mean, did you … umm, clean up the spaghetti I dropped?" I asked swallowing heavily.

Even after I asked her this, I knew she didn't have enough time to clean it up with the little time I was outside.

She looked behind me at the steaming pot of water almost ready to boil over. "Not sure what you mean?" Laughing to herself, she sauntered over to the stove, her eyes fixed on the simmering marinara sauce. Placing her book firmly under her armpit, she reached for another piece of bread and proceeded to dunk it into the tangy sauce. With a satisfied grin on her face, she took a bite, allowing the flavors of her mother's family recipe, that we all adored, to explode in her mouth. She let out a long, contented moan, taking in all the rich spices. Her face was a picture of pure bliss and happiness. "You've copied your grandma's recipe perfectly. Don't forget to take your brother a plate," she said, patting me on the head and sauntering out of the room. She poked her nose back in the book while finishing off her pre-dinner snack.

From that night on, a whole new world had opened to me, one where I possessed the extraordinary ability to go back in time. I became absolutely obsessed with this newfound power, and I found myself trying it out every single chance I got. As I dug deeper into the mystery of it all, I couldn't help but wonder if there were others out there who possessed this remarkable ability.

This curiosity drove me to scrutinize every person, familiar and unfamiliar, that I came into contact with. I examined them intently for any signs that they too could travel through time. Though I wasn't entirely sure what I was searching for, I couldn't resist the urge to investigate. I began noticing things I'd never paid attention to before. I saw the tiny freckles that speckled people's eyelids and earlobes, the slight crookedness of their teeth, and the subtle beauty that lay hidden in every single face I encountered. It struck me how many years I had spent simply going through the motions of my daily life without truly looking at the people around me.

In my quest for answers, I decided to do some research on the manufacturer of the swing set, hoping to find someone, anyone, who could shed some light on my insane situation. But as I pondered over what I would actually ask this person, a creeping sense of doubt began gnawing at me, making me wonder if I was slowly but surely losing my grip on reality.

I made it a habit to test out my powers every single day, swinging away any occurrence that I could think of, not just the unpleasant ones. I was consumed with the need to seek out whether I still possessed this power or not, and I couldn't bear the thought of waking up one day and realizing it had vanished from me overnight.

Painting bright, awful make-up all over my face like a clown heading off to a preschooler's birthday party, I'd run out to the swing and wish for the moment right before. It never stopped fascinating me when things went back to the time I wished them to go back to. Once, I got ballsy and threw the only good dinner plate we own—one of the only ones Ponyboy hadn't caused one of us to drop or chip—to the ground and watched it shatter. Sure enough, after going outside and swinging away, I came inside, and the plate with its beautiful pearl, shimmered rim was as good as new, sitting in the cupboard like it hadn't been touched.

As I continued to swing back and forth, I found myself experimenting with the limits of my powers. I attempted to conjure up vivid images of my ideal future, envisioning Frankie and I living in California by Rafa, while I pursued my journalism degree and Frankie his nursing career. To be with Rafa again would make all of this so much easier on me mentally. Best friends are a must when you realize you can time travel, and mine moved to California.

Nothing seemed to happen when I thought about the future, and I didn't want to be guilty of wishful thinking, but I couldn't help but feel curious about what parts of my future were within my control. My experiments with time travel had taught me that while I could go back and relive the past, my future was entirely up to me to make happen.

In a way, this served as a reassuring safety measure, reminding me that ultimately, my destiny lay in my own hands. The swing set time machine god—whatever that is—had perhaps put this in place for a reason, ensuring I didn't become too dependent on my powers and lose sight of who I was before this craziness started.

Although the temptation to meddle with world events was strong, I knew deep down that this was a line I shouldn't cross. The idea of altering the course of events for complete strangers felt inherently wrong to me.

My goal was to change the events of my own past, to make things right in my brother's life. But even then, I was aware that my actions could have far-reaching consequences that extended beyond my own life. Once I went back in time, there was no turning back.

The thought of sharing my secret with anyone, even those closest to me, filled me with a sense of anxiety. What if that was the key to losing this ability? I didn't know if there were any hard and fast rules that governed time travel, but the thought of tempting fate by telling my secret was a risk I wasn't willing to take, not yet anyway. And that was the scariest part. Making this tough decision for my brother could really screw things up if I was wrong and that would fall solely on me. The choice to help Jojo, to change the course of his fate, would ultimately have to be made by me alone without any input from my family or Frankie.

I somehow already knew I was going to lose things that meant everything to me for the good of Jojo. This power came with a heavy burden. I knew, deep down, that to help my brother, I'd have to make sacrifices that would be painful and difficult. The knowledge that I could alter the course of events that had caused my brother's injury and all the pain he'd endured was both exhilarating and terrifying.

If I was going to go back and change something major like this, I had to be one hundred percent sure I was okay with the outcome. How does any seventeen-year-old know anything for sure? The one thing I did know was that Jojo was going to eat himself to death and never escape the dungeon of his bedroom if I didn't do something to help. What I didn't know was how it would change things for me and Frankie, the complete love of my life.

Chapter Two

The sound of Frankie's jeep horn echoes through the house from the driveway, signaling his arrival, as I carefully make my way up the stairs to deliver Jojo his breakfast. The plate I'm carrying is delicately balanced, its contents of fluffy eggs and whole wheat toast practically teetering on the edge as I hurry to reach Frankie's car.

Even though I'm aware that my brother is probably getting sick of having eggs for breakfast every day, I refuse to serve him the sugary calorie-laden cakes my mom or Justine brings him as a way of pacifying him. Instead, I provide him with a healthy breakfast in my effort to get him out of being stuck inside the same four walls all day. What Jojo really needs is an opportunity to escape, not just a temporary mental escape through sweets.

I set the plate of eggs on Jojo's nightstand amongst candy bar wrappers and empty soda cans. Looking down, I realize I forgot to bring his Flintstone vitamin upstairs with me. It's silly, really, but my mom insists we take one every morning. Jojo and I are too old for them, but we humor her anyways. The purple Dino one with its sweet grape sourness is my favorite—it's childish, I know. Hearing me come in, he turns his head toward the plate and rolls his body slightly sideways. The pain I see etched across his face every morning is there and it's soul crushing.

"I can't do eggs again," he says with his disheveled bangs dipping into his eyes like a shaggy dog.

He needs a haircut. The last time he had one, it was my mom who took it upon herself to do the job with nothing but a pair of kitchen scissors and a towel to collect the fallen hair. My brother promised her he would handle it on his own from then on, but the tangled mess of hair before me is evidence of his neglect.

"You can and you will do eggs again." I place my hands on my hips to remind him I'm in charge of his meals now. I feel like a fraud trying to command him into following my orders. As his younger sister, I've always been aware of the unspoken rule that he's the one in charge of enforcing family guidelines. It seems to be a universal pecking order amongst siblings, with the oldest always holding a certain level of authority over the younger ones. I can't think of a single family where this pecking order doesn't exist to some extent.

He reaches over and crinkles the empty candy wrappers with his meaty fingers before he looks at the plate with all the excitement of a kid who was just handed a geometry test.

"Seriously? Who is bringing you this crap?" I ask him, swooshing all the wrappers into the trash can beside his bed. I count at least six candy bar wrappers in there before the new ones land on top of them in this junk food wrapper graveyard.

He gives me a long, slow scowl, but his verbal response remains absent. I can't figure out whether it's my mom or Justine who's providing him with this unhealthy junk. As for my dad, he's not contributing to this culinary chaos because he shares my belief that we should be giving Jojo healthy meals ... or at least I think he does. However, my dad hesitates to deliver any healthy meals to Jojo because he doesn't want to disappoint him. I think it's cowardly of him, but my dad always tends to lead with his heart, a trait I used to admire, until now. We need some tough love in this house and I'm the only one giving it.

Justine and Jojo have been together for three

years, starting from when he was a star football player during his junior year in high school. I have to give Justine credit for staying with Jojo despite the fact that he can no longer fit through his bedroom doorway, let alone take her out on a real date or go anywhere with her for that matter. It's not like they can go to parties or hang out with their friends, and that has to be difficult for both of them. Justine loves Jojo for who he is, not what he looks like, which is exactly what anyone would want for their loved ones. Each and every one of us deserves love based on the essence of who we are on the inside, rather than our external appearance. I need her support because this new plan to help my brother is going to be tough on all of us, and I can say without a doubt that at least she's not a shallow asshole like most teenagers I know.

It doesn't help that our old house is a relic of the past, constructed with doorways so narrow that even a slim person barely fits through them. Trying to walk through one of our doorways with a laundry basket takes some maneuvering and we've all been knocked backwards trying to rush into a room with one. As it turns out, the homes on our street were built in a time when people were smaller, a tidbit of information we learned from my dad's research at the local library.

The realization was both funny and perplexing as we contemplated the possibility of being descendants of tiny ancestors. Our neighbor Mr. Strand had to pay a ton of money to widen all the doorways in his home to make room for his wife's walker after she suffered a stroke. It was a massive undertaking that made us appreciate the challenges of accommodating individuals with disabilities in older homes even more.

What I don't understand is why the hell Justine continues making it harder on me to help Jojo to get some of this weight off. It's not just about his excess weight—

the problem is that he can't leave his room. Apparently, I'm the only person who can provide my brother with the kind of tough love he needs to change his lifestyle. Justine, on the other hand, seems to be coddling him with an overly indulgent, almost sickeningly sweet form of love that could ultimately lead to his death in that dank cave of his room. But I won't let that happen, and I'm going to stop it before we get to a path of no return—even though we seem to already be there.

Sliding my brother's heavy, grey curtains open, I give him my customary morning pat on the leg as I wave to Frankie out the window, so he at least knows I'm coming. And without any clear motive, Ponyboy appears and thrusts himself between my legs, causing me to lose my balance. My right hand lands directly in the salsa on my brother's plate. I do give him salsa with his eggs, I'm strict, but not a monster.

"Good one." He laughs, and his bed creaks and shakes like a bowl of gelatin riding on top of a moving car. It seems to be jiggling more than it did even a month ago and that can't be good on the floor either. It's good to see him laugh. I just wish it wasn't at me in this moment.

"Shut it, Jojo."

Ridding my hand of the tomato and onions stuck to it with a tissue and rushing to get outside, I wonder how long Jojo's bed is going to hold up even with the reinforced two-by-fours my dad installed not even six months ago. The uncomfortable and awkward situation that arose from having to repair the bed with my brother still in it has created a lingering sadness between my dad and Jojo that has yet to be resolved. My dad was used to throwing a football around in the back yard with Jojo while they contemplated how the Kansas City Chiefs were doing, not fixing his bed so it could hold his weight. In the beginning, my dad tried helping Jojo out of this funk, but it caused arguments, and my dad isn't good with confrontation.

Like a pole vaulter, I hoist myself into Frankie's jeep, hoping we aren't too late. "So sorry, we're gonna be late … again."

He gives me the sympathetic smile he's been giving me the last three years. Let's face it, I've always run behind for everything even before I started making Jojo's meals. Late people suck, and I'm one of them.

"It's okay. I know it's for a good cause," he says as he glances up at my brother's window, giving my arm a squeeze.

I usually prepare all of Jojo's meals the night before, but last night I fell asleep on the couch after watching a new episode of Family Ties with my dad. I must admit Alex P. Keaton's character is self-absorbed on the show and I don't care for his opinions, but his ambition and heart are growing on me more and more with every episode.

Despite my best intentions to get up early and prepare Jojo a hot lunch that Justine could bring to his room after her first three classes were over, I slept through my blaring alarm clock. Instead, I had to resort to making him a turkey and veggie sandwich like I've been doing most days lately. I do take some peace in the fact that I was able to at least cook up some eggs this morning. It's a small yet welcome change to his routine I implemented last week that he's already tired of. Well, if it were me, I would welcome the change even though he'd rather have a box of donuts. I'm beginning to feel increasingly irritated and worn out from this whole mess. I want to start seeing some improvement without swinging back and really shaking everything up.

So here I am, late, with salsa in my fingernails. I could've gone outside and cranked myself back and forth on the swing to start this whole day over, but I've learned that sometimes the new version of my day can be worse than the one I wanted to redo. It can be an endless cycle of starting over that becomes maddening and can get quite confusing and exhausting.

"Well, if it helps, you look beautiful as usual," he says.

I lean over to plant a tender kiss on his lips and breathe in the delightful fragrance of roasted coffee beans that seems to permeate his clothing. He works at Dunkin' Donuts before school, and the smell of sweet donuts and coffee swirling in his jeep always brings me comfort. My family is obsessed with donuts—who doesn't love a glazed donut slathered with chocolate frosting. I now have them banned from entering our house. My dad would never be able to resist the temptation of taking one up to Jojo.

My dad and Jojo loved to sit on my mom's porch swing on a Saturday morning with a box of donuts between them before my mom and I were even up. A lot of our family traditions are centered around food, and we've lost that. Looking at that porch swing now brings about so much sadness. I don't think my dad has sat on it in years now that Jojo can't physically be outside with him.

"How's it going with your brother?" Frankie pulls out of my driveway slowly even though we're in a rush.

"Well since I have no way of knowing what he weighs because, you know, we don't have a scale that size, I'm not sure."

I think for a minute for any telltale signs of weight loss when I caught a glimpse of him earlier this morning. My view was obstructed by the shabby and worn-out Kansas City Chiefs bedspread my mom bought him a couple of Christmas's ago that he habitually keeps wrapped around his body, revealing nothing below his chest.

To help him with a daily hygiene routine, my mom thoughtfully leaves soap, water, and a fresh towel on his bedside table every day. Jojo and I have a shared bathroom, but I have no clue if he can get into it. He's adamant about maintaining his privacy, as evidenced by his decision to lock the door that once allowed me to enter the bathroom from my room over a year ago. I now have to use the hallway bathroom, further cementing the established hierarchy among siblings. Again, there's a pecking order with siblings, and I lose.

The familiar sensation of tears creates a film over my eyes as I think about what his life has become, and I swallow the closed off ache in my throat. This is not who Jojo is nor what any of us thought would happen after a football injury ruined his chances of ever playing again. Football was everything to him, and we've all watched as he has tried fighting off the depression sinking into him like a man trying to walk through quicksand. It just took over his way of life. No longer was he in the gym before and after school. He could barely walk after his leg surgery.

"Well, if he's been eating all those diet recipes you're finding in your magazines, it has to be doing something," he says, trying to sound encouraging.

I nod guiltily because I've been slacking on making those meals, opting for the easier eggs, sandwiches, and fruit and veggies route. I need to refocus my efforts.

He looks at me, and his pale, blue eyes and black hair are still such a stunning contrast to me that I hold my breath for a second. Despite having stared into those eyes countless times over the years, I still find myself entranced by their beauty, as if I'm being pulled in by an irresistible magnetic force.

"I know, right? But I think he's making Justine feel bad for him, or maybe it's my parents I'm not sure, but I found empty candy wrappers in his room and an empty bottle of soda for God's sake."

"Surely Justine wouldn't dare derail your plan."

Nodding, I know he's not even joking when he says this.

I held a family meeting exactly one month ago including Justine and Frankie. If Jojo is the love of Justine's life like she says he is, she needed to be in on the new strategy to save Jojo from the awful existence he has going on in that prison cell of a bedroom. The mere fact that we all had to crowd into Jojo's bedroom to hold the family meeting should be the kick in the ass my family needed to help Jojo.

We sat in a circle, shoulder to shoulder, on his bedroom floor like we were at a slumber party telling secrets nobody outside the circle was allowed to know while my brother glared at us from his bed. Frankie was there for moral support, and he even helped me create handwritten notes for me to share with my family prior to the meeting. Justine played with a loose piece of carpet the entire time with zero input while my parents just nodded in response to anything I said.

That night I passed Jojo's room as he sat hunched against his wall shrouded in darkness, playing Donkey Kong with tears running down his cheeks. I didn't have to ask him what was wrong. Seeing my family pass by his room going about our normal routines of work and school day after day was killing him, and I knew it was time for a change. I was going to force us all into some sort of plan even if they all ended up hating me for it.

"That's no good. We need to find out where the snacks are coming from and put a stop to it for sure." He finally backs onto the street with a frown on his face.

I'm truly grateful for the unwavering support Frankie has shown me ever since I confided in him about my new plan to help Jojo. Of course, he has no idea that I can swing back and fix it all. I try not to think about how he'd feel about me going back to save my brother from this crisis. Would he support the fact that I didn't want to let go of what he and I had? Or would his nature of wanting to help anyone kick in, and he'd be ashamed that he was in love with someone who selfishly didn't want to change it all immediately for Jojo? I feel ashamed anytime my mind wanders to what he'd do. I guess I know the answer deep down.

He has been an absolute godsend, helping me in every possible way to ensure that my plan for Jojo's weight loss is executed perfectly. From scouring through numerous culinary magazines at the library in search of recipes that are both nutritious and delicious, so Jojo doesn't feel deprived, to coming up with a comprehensive workout routine he learned from his health care studies at school for someone who is confined to bed due to a long-term injury, his efforts have been nothing short of amazing. His help means everything to me. I couldn't have done any of this without him, especially now that Rafa is in California.

"Yeah, I plan to corner Justine tonight. I'll know the minute I see her if she's guilty," I say.

"Try to go easy on her. She loves him, too."

"Sometimes I wonder about that. If you were in this situation, I'd do everything in my power to help you." I look at him and it's true. There's no way I'd bring him junk food and watch him continue to deteriorate because of something I was doing for him.

"I understand that, but we don't know what it's like to be in her shoes. I believe she wants him to be happy and that's where her focus is. You can't blame her for that."

He grabs my hand and intertwines our fingers, which would normally calm me down when I'm feeling frustrated about my brother's situation, but not today.

Frankie's ability to stay so objective in this situation sometimes makes me a little crazy. Why can't he just agree that Justine's being ridiculous? These are the moments when I need Rafa with me. Rafa would agree with me even if it was just to make me feel better—or shut me up.

The stakes are higher than Frankie could possibly imagine. As I gaze over at him, I find myself struggling to push aside the terrifying possibility of losing the happiness he has brought into my life. If Jojo fails to make progress in shedding this weight, all the cherished moments Frankie and I have shared over the past three years will be wiped clean, as if they never even existed. How can I possibly recapture all the moments that caused us to fall in love?

The memories that formed our relationship will fade into oblivion. They'll only be left in my memory, not his. I'm just hoping we can help Jojo without having to forfeit the special moments that have defined the last three years of my life. The weight of this burden is almost too much to bear, and I can only hope that our plan starts working and soon.

I'm hesitant to act on any other strategy than the one we're working on. I've been trying to prepare myself to make the biggest sacrifice of my life, but I refuse to do so without putting up a fight. I know deep down I'm Jojo's sister, and I owe it to him to honor that bond. But the uncertainty over whether I can go back to that fateful night on the football field when Jojo's leg was crushed and alter the course of events is another thing keeping me from going back. Can one person cause such a drastic change? These questions torment me as I contemplate my next move.

Going back for Jojo could ruin everything I love about my life, and it's looking like that's exactly what I'm going to have to do if he doesn't get better.

CARRIE BEAMER

Chapter Three

Frankie, our high school's mascot, was none other than the Mighty Dogger—a gigantic wiener dog that represented our school in a way that was somewhat absurd but strangely endearing at the same time. Nobody really knew who chose this mascot for our school long ago, but there was a certain charm to it I couldn't deny. Who didn't love a wiener dog? The unfortunate part was that the football team had taken to calling themselves the Mighty Wieners, which was obviously ridiculous. The parents let it be known that they didn't care for the inappropriateness of the wiener reference, but that just eggs them all on.

It was at a party hosted by Dax Goulart, the quarterback of our school's football team, where I first met Frankie, the charming boy behind the Mighty Dogger suit. We'd all just come from a deflating football game. Watching my brother's team lose a game they could've easily won had Jojo been playing left us all feeling down in the dumps. We all knew our star running back could've changed the outcome, but I couldn't imagine what it was like for Jojo to know it.

I was largely known as Jojo Ortega's younger sister, which was not surprising given he was a senior while I was just a freshman. Jojo was the star athlete of our high school, and he'd been on the radar of college scouts until three weeks prior when his leg was shattered in two places following a nasty tackle against the Ruskin Eagles who were known to play dirty. The tackle was so bad it prompted my dad—who is the most mild-mannered person anyone knows—to charge onto the field red faced while shouting a string of cuss words I didn't even know he knew. If Joseph Sr is charging a football field someone had majorly wronged someone he loved.

The football team convinced me to bring Jojo to the party, promising me the team comradery would lift his spirits. However, it quickly became apparent their plan had backfired. As I sat by myself in a lawn chair, observing the crowd gathered around the grill all wearing their orange and black football jerseys with shorts, I could see all the players attempting to cheer up Jojo with their football stories. In hindsight, I realized this was probably not the best idea. Listening to stories of his former glory, when he was now struggling to even walk, had to be devastating for Jojo. I watched as the smoke from the grill wafted over everyone and the smell of smoky burgers and charcoal made my mouth water. I was reluctant to join the line of people waiting for food for fear Jojo would catch sight of me and let me know how pissed he was I brought him here.

Driving his truck without a driver's license to get him there was scarier than I thought it'd be. That truck was like a tank, and Jojo blaring Motley Crew on his tape deck made it even harder to concentrate. My parents wouldn't be happy about the fact that I drove, but when it came to helping Jojo they tended to look past certain rules.

"Hey, can you do me a huge favor and hold my head?" a muffled voice asked from behind me.

I turned to see the Mighty Dogger in all his furry dog glory.

Being confronted by a giant wiener dog, its teeth bared and snarling as if ready to pounce, was alarming to say the least. Whoever created this costume had managed to perfectly capture the ferocity of a dog's expression right before it sinks its teeth into you. This definitely killed the nostalgic end of summer BBQ vibe I was feeling. In order to create some space between my face and the intimidating pile of fur, I scooted my patio chair back quickly, causing a loud metal chair on cement scraping noise to ring out across the patio. Before I knew it, I was tumbling to the ground with my legs flailing in the air. The person inside the Mighty Dogger costume rushed to help me back onto my feet. This was embarrassing to say the least.

I couldn't blame this one on Ponyboy.

"Oh my gosh are you okay?" he asked through the dog head before he threw it off.

It landed with a thump on the ground next to us. That thing sounded like it weighed a ton. Staring down at it, I wondered how his neck held it up. I glanced up to inspect his neck—I was in a bit of a daze. Struck by this sweaty boys' intense eyes, I couldn't answer him right away. I felt wobbly as he gently grabbed my wrist and lead me inside to sit on the couch with a crowd of kids, including my brother, staring after us like we just somehow ruined the party. He didn't notice the gawking looks, which was a relief.

"You hit your head really hard," he said and then he ran out of the living room on a mission.

The sight of him running in the wiener dog suit across the living room was funny to me. Mascots are typically designed for sports fields, not for a domestic setting. Just as I was wondering where the heck he ran off to, he reappeared, sprinting back into the room with a bag of frozen corn in his hand.

"Here, let me feel the back of your head," he said, sliding closer to me.

I flinched a little as he brought a big furry paw toward me.

"Oh right, I should probably take this off first." He rid himself of the giant wiener by standing up and shimming his hips side to side, and I almost blushed.

"I'm okay, really. This head is used to being knocked about." I laughed at myself, wishing I could run and hide. Suddenly, every word I thought to say made me seem like a complete weirdo.

"I'm in the EMT work program at school and head injuries are nothing to take lightly."

Sitting beside me in black basketball shorts and a Beastie Boys t-shirt, he was a sweaty mess from the dog suit, but surprisingly, he didn't reek of sweat and grime. As someone who had grown accustomed to the pungent odor of my brother's post-football practice smell of chili and sloppy joes, I was grateful that his scent was nonexistent. He leaned back and ran his hand over the back of my head, checking for any bumps. I didn't know what to do, so I just let him go about his inspection of my head with my hands planted in my lap.

"Did you drive here in that thing?" I asked, looking down at the pile of fluffy mascot pieces on the floor, trying to keep my breathing steady while he touched me and fill the silence of his concentration.

"What? Oh, no. I put it on when I got here. I don't think I could or should drive in it." He gave a small laugh.

With his eyes narrowed on my head, he focused all his attention on me. I turned around so he could carefully slide his fingers back and forth through my hair, checking for an injury I couldn't feel anymore. The sensation that coursed through me was like that of a doctor's gentle touch with a stethoscope as I breathed in and out. It was strange, but the feeling was comforting in a way I couldn't put into words. I recalled the same tranquil sensation when Rafa used to delicately comb through my hair on the bus, lulling me into a blissful state of relaxation. I could've drifted off to sleep in that moment, feeling oddly at ease.

"Well, I think your head's okay, but you should still put this on it," he said, softly settling the frozen bag of corn onto the crown of my head while looking directly into my eyes, inspecting them for abnormalities I guessed. It made my heart speed up with him looking at me so intently.

I gave in and took over with the bag of corn, knowing I didn't need it, but I could tell it was important to him that I used it. The EMT program at school must be no joke if he took injuries this seriously.

"So why were you in the dog suit?" I asked him. I wanted to take the attention off me for a minute before I had a heart attack from all the feelings I was experiencing.

"I was going to surprise the team and try to cheer them up after the loss tonight. But then I got here and realized that was a lame idea." He glanced down at the abandoned pile of dog fur and shook his head at the costume like it had personally offended him.

This made me laugh. "I don't think it's lame at all. I think it shows damn good school spirit," I said, and I genuinely meant it.

As someone who lacks coordination, I'd always admired school spirit from a distance. The idea of being part of the marching band or cheerleading squad sounded good, but I knew I didn't have what it took to do either. Even my cat seemed to recognize my lack of agility, making me the easiest target in the house for his attacks. I'd found my niche in writing, and I channeled my school pride into articles for the newspaper and yearbook. It occurred to me I'd never written a story about our school mascot, but that was about to change. This guy deserved a spotlight in our yearbook.

He grinned at me. "You might be the only one to think that."

I returned the smile, unsure if it was safe to remove the corn from my head or not, but my arm was getting tired of holding it up.

"I'm Frankie. Frankie Rubio, by the way." He put his hand out for me to shake.

I thought it was cute how formal he was about introducing himself after he just ran his hands through my hair and stared into my eyes as if my life depended on it.

"Dessy Ortega," I said and shook his hand, finally having an excuse to drop the bag of corn to my lap.

"Oh cool, so your Jojo's sister?"

"That would be me." I leaned back into the couch so I could crisscross my legs and act causal.

"I'm sorry about what happened to your brother. He was an amazing player. I bet it's been rough on you, too."

The inclusion of me in his apology about my brother's injury was touching. He was right. It's been hard on my whole family.

"Yeah, he's been a beast at football since he could walk practically. Funny he has a sister that can't even sit in a chair without falling." I shook my head and laughed at myself once again.

"That's my fault. You were sitting just fine until I came up and startled you. Sorry about that by the way."

"If you hang around me long enough, I can't guarantee that it won't happen again. The night is young and guys in dog costumes can jump out from anywhere." I couldn't help but smile at him as I held my hands up and wiggled my fingers in his face.

"To be honest, hanging around you has been the best part of my night. Wearing that sweat trap tonight on the field was suffocating and I'm starving." He looked over at me. "Have you had a burger yet?"

"No, I was just about to get one before I was attacked by a dog." I laughed and peered out to the patio where Mr. Goulart was manning the grill.

"If you stay here and put this back on your head, I'll go out and get us both a burger. It's the least I can do." He picked up the bag of corn and put it in my hand. I could tell he felt sincerely responsible for my head landing on the pavement out back.

"You have a deal," I said. The fact that I could sit on the couch while he got me a plate of food, saving me from a patio of rowdy football players, made up for my not very injured head.

"Ketchup? Mustard?" he asked as he got up.

"Both. Oh, and can you see if they have pickles?"

I liked my burgers fully loaded, and I wasn't ashamed to admit it.

"You can't have a burger without pickles. Well, you could, but why would you? I'll be right back."

As I watched him walk outside, I felt like I'd just met the nicest guy I'd ever known. I'd only known him for like ten minutes, but I could tell in that little amount of time that he wasn't a jerk. It wasn't like some weird intense love thing—I just really liked his energy.

It wasn't even his looks that got me, although, I had to admit the boy had good hair. It was black and messy and rose and fell in all the right ways. And that was after wearing a big dog head on it all night. His eyes were exotic and beautiful, but that wasn't it. His demeanor was what pulled me in.

I'd never felt as at ease and content as I did talking with Frankie, aside from Rafa, who moved to live with an aunt who had surfaced in his life after years of being in foster care. Rafa's mother, a single parent with no family or so we thought, had died from a rare form of cancer when he was only six, and no one had come forward to claim him because nobody knew about him besides his birth father.

Rafa eventually learned that his mother had left home to be with his father, who had turned out to be an irresponsible man and had abandoned them both. She was too ashamed to return home after running away and becoming pregnant. After Rafa moved away, I felt lost but also relieved he finally had a family to call his own, in addition to me, of course.

"This night is looking up," Frankie said, walking in holding two plates loaded down with food. "They had ketchup, mustard, and pickles, but check this out." He set one of the plates on my lap and plopped down beside me. "They also had spears." He looked so proud of the pickle spear he was holding up.

"Perfect," I said, nodding.

"They also had chicken wings. Do you want me to go back and get you some?"

"Nah, I'm good. The macaroni and cheese you got me looks much better than a chicken wing." I smiled at his willingness to go back out there for me.

"I like them, but I don't like eating messy food with my hands. It seems sort of gross," he said.

"That's how I feel too. Unless it's a pickle."

I picked mine up and he tapped his pickle spear to mine in cheers.

Finally, I thought, *a nice guy to talk to*. I was done dealing with my brother's friends. I didn't fit in with them, but I thought I could fit in with Frankie.

Chapter Four

As Frankie pulls up to drop me off after another long day at school, I see Justine's old, brown rusted out clunker parked beside Jojo's truck, which has remained unused by Jojo since the fateful day he was injured. I remember my dad had to drive it back from the hospital, after he'd followed the ambulance that took my brother off the field. Jojo's cassette tapes still lay untouched on the dashboard, collecting dust as their cover jackets fade under the relentless sun.

I've never dared to ask, but I've always secretly longed to drive his truck like it was my own now. Normally, I rely on Frankie or Justine to drive me around, as my parents can't afford another car. It would feel wrong asking my brother about using his truck, given his circumstances. It would be a slap in the face to his situation, but maybe I need to start pushing for things like this and hope they change his will to get out of bed.

"Well look who's not at work. Justine and I are about to have a serious talk," I say, lowering my eyes at the house, prepared for battle.

"Remember to go easy on her. She's just trying to make him happy like anyone would want for him right now," Frankie says, echoing his speech to me this morning and leaning in for a kiss.

"Yeah, well, there's plenty of ways to make a person happy without ruining their health."

"I can't really disagree with you on that."

As I kiss his lips softly, he immediately pulls me closer, intensifying the moment with a longer, more lingering kiss. I feel myself surrendering to his touch, my body melting as I press myself against him, reveling in the sweet and intoxicating sensation of his lips on mine.

The mere thought of losing him is overwhelming, and I wish this moment could last forever.

I quickly snap out of it, pulling away to focus on the task ahead of me. I'm on a mission. I need to get in there and remind Justine why we need to help Jojo.

"She must be stopped," I say, opening the jeep door. I give him one more kiss on the cheek and hop out of his jeep in a steady conquer the world manner.

"Are we still on for a burger after you get his dinner made?"

Frankie and I get a burger at our favorite burger joint every Monday night. Mondays at Pete's Drive-In is two-for-one burger night, and we love to go and get a burger—with extra pickles of course. It's our way of connecting before a busy week of school, activities, and work ahead.

"Absolutely, wouldn't miss it."

As I shut the door to his jeep, I turn back to gaze at him, my heart bursting with affection for him. His beaming smile mirrors mine, and I can't help but feel like the luckiest girl in the world. We were friends for a couple of months before we fell in love. We met in August and fell in love during the course of that first fall. How can you not fall in love during a Midwest autumn? In Missouri, fall means football, crisp weather, and the satisfying crunch of leaves beneath your feet. It's the season of cozy sweaters, pumpkin-spiced coffees, romantic walks, and long conversations on the phone all night while cuddled up in piles of blankets with the cool wind howling outside your window. He brought a magical quality to my days that I never knew I was missing, and I couldn't imagine ever being without him.

He rolls the window down and says, "I love you, Des. Good luck."

"I love you too. Thanks, I'll need it!"

Taking a moment to tuck my hair behind my ears, I steel myself for the task ahead—dealing with Justine. With my parents due to come home soon, I know I need to act fast to catch her alone, without my mom coming to her rescue.

As I step into the house, my eyes immediately fall on Justine. She's perched on the kitchen counter, seemingly waiting for me. Scooping up Ponyboy from the floor to prevent him from getting in my way, my heart jumps out of my chest as I get a closer look at her. I'm so flustered I drop Ponyboy to the ground. Ignoring his loud meow of protest, I try refocusing my eyes on Justine. "Justine! What the…"

As I take in the sight before me, my breathing quickens, and my brain struggles to process what I'm seeing. There she is standing in front of me in a stunning spaghetti-strapped pink, satin prom dress, but my initial awe was quickly replaced with horror. Every inch of her dress is covered with streaks of blood, making my stomach churn with anxiety even though I know it can't be real. My mind is playing tricks on the rest of me.

"I'm Carrie. You know, from the movie *Carrie*," she says, gesturing up and down at the blood-covered dress she has on in a lackadaisical manner.

"Dear God, is this one of my mom's new ones?" For the briefest of seconds, I thought she had stumbled in the house after some sort of violent attack or something else that would probably never happen in my quiet, tree lined, old neighborhood. I don't know what I'd thought, but it scared the hell out of me.

She nods her head and saunters across the kitchen to pull something out of the beeping microwave.

My parents saved for a long time to buy a microwave, and Justine seems to use it more than they do. I think my mom's afraid of it. She'll get a pan out just to heat up soup even though we've shown her several times how to just pop her bowl in the microwave.

Justine nods and stands back away from it when it's running like it might explode. "There's a bloody tiara that goes with it too. It's pretty cool. I just came from the shop. Your mom wanted me to bring the dress here so she could sew some sequins on it tonight. I should've probably changed first," she says, taking the bowl of noodles she just pulled out of the microwave over to the counter. "Can you imagine if a cop pulled me over and I was wearing this?" She smiled but went right back to her usual sullen expression.

I can't stop staring at her. The blood looks so real. My brain knows the blood is fake, but I can't seem to calm down when looking at her. Good job, Mom. Wow.

My parents are the proud owners of a quaint little costume shop that's been a staple in downtown Kansas City for as long as I can remember. Ortega Costumes and Props is their pride and joy, and they've poured their hearts and souls into making it a thriving business. As the name suggests, they specialize in renting and selling costumes of all kinds, from classic movie characters to futuristic sci-fi ensembles. But what sets them apart is their unique service of renting out prom and formal dresses, a popular choice among teenagers looking to make a statement without breaking the bank.

My parents are well-known around town, not just for their quirky costumes but for their exceptional customer service and expertise. It's not uncommon to see them strolling down the streets of Kansas City, decked out in costumes ranging from Sonny and Cher to Bonnie and Clyde, all in the name of promoting their beloved business. I'm always amazed at the sheer number of people who come through our doors, even outside of Halloween season. The local theater productions frequently enlist my mom's help with costume design for their musicals and plays, a testament to her creative talents and eye for detail. She's such an amazing seamstress. I don't have the patience for it.

I have to say, I really dig my parents' quirkiness. Most kids would probably be embarrassed by them, but they're living their dream and I think it's pretty kick ass. Also, growing up, Jojo and I had the best costumes to trick-or-treat in. I could feel the jealousy a mile away when other kids saw us. One year I went as E.T., and my mom made the most epic alien costume. I looked like I came right from the movie onto our block.

Justine and I both work at the shop on the weekends, but sometimes Justine goes in after school to try on my mom's new creations. Justine's perfect for it because she's average height whereas I'm only five foot one. I'm perfect when it comes to trying on some of the kids' costumes—the E.T. costume still fits me.

Justine cuts a chunk of the soft butter from the flowered, porcelain butter dish on our kitchen table and slides it in the bowl of warm noodles. As she turns to open the fridge, I clench both my fists at my side and ask her what she's making with rage growing inside me.

"Oh, I'm just making Jojo some healthy macaroni and cheese for a snack. He's hungry and just wanted something before you have his dinner ready." She tries to say this nonchalantly, but her voice betrays her. She pulls a bag of shredded cheese out of the fridge, and I see a slight tremble in her hands. She knows I'm going to flip out. There's no way she believes what she's making is healthy, as she's studying to be a nurse someday. Butter and noodles healthy? No way.

"First of all, we both know there's nothing healthy about that bowl of fat-laden grease you've got going there, and second, I have a whole shelf in the fridge set aside for his snacks."

I'm trying to keep my tone even, but the longer I stare at the bowl of thick noodles swimming in butter, the madder I'm getting. My mind is on a constant reminder loop that the outcome of this last-ditch effort to get Jojo out of his room and back to real life is my whole future with Frankie.

She looks down at the bag of shredded cheese in her hand, but she doesn't move or make eye contact with me. Justine isn't good at one-on-one conflict. She folds like a tent with no poles in a windstorm the minute someone questions her.

"Look, see right here?" I say, pointing to a shelf in the fridge with hard boiled eggs, various chopped up veggies, olives, and some sliced apples. "These are his snacks, or he can have some of these nuts," I say, stomping over to the counter and holding up the bag of nuts I bought for Jojo last weekend and shaking them at her. Richard Simmons says nuts are the perfect snack for a balanced diet and he should know—he has transformed his whole life. But dang nuts are expensive. Jojo better eat them. My mom wasn't happy that this bag of nuts sucked up some of our grocery money.

"I know, I'm sorry. I agree with you. I hate when he asks me to make him something like that," she says, gesturing to the pasta. "He's miserable enough without me arguing with him about his diet, so that's why I just do it."

"When he asks, tell him no and walk away for a minute. Don't engage in an argument about it. Toughen up and take a stand, Justine." I fold my arms over my chest. "Did you bring him the chocolate and the soda?"

She looks out across the living room as if she wants to run away from me, and it's hard to be firm with a sweet blonde wearing a blood covered prom dress. She looks like she just barely escaped with her life already.

"Hello?" I lean in and look her dead in the face.

"Yeah, he called me at the shop and asked me to bring it yesterday," she says quietly, like a child being scolded for eating junk before dinner.

"Have you lost your mind? Why are you helping him stay in this state of never-ending depression? You say you love him, but…"

"That's why, Dessy," she says, surprisingly interrupting me. "He's so depressed, and it's killing me to see him like this. The only thing that makes him smile anymore is food. Food he likes. All I want is for him to be happy." She puts her face in her hands, and I know she's crying.

Frankie nailed it—she just wants him to be happy. I'm not trying to be heartless, but at some point, everyone needs to stop catering to Jojo's requests for rubbish. Junk food doesn't even help him feel full. But I know deep down it's not about the food for him—it's never been about the food.

"I get it, okay? It breaks your heart to see him so unhappy, and you just want him to find some joy in his life now that he's stuck. It's breaking all our hearts, Justine, but simply bringing him junk food is only a temporary solution to his sadness. You know deep down that what he really needs is a permanent change that can bring him true happiness.

"What would you tell one of your patients someday? We have to help him get thin enough to at least step out of his room so he will finally see all the amazing things he has been missing out on while being stuck in there." I point my thumb behind me toward Jojo's room, and she flinches. "Don't you understand that? We have to get him out of there." I slam my hand on the kitchen counter, and she drops her hands and looks down, but she doesn't move.

I dump the bowl of macaroni in the trash and open the fridge back up. I grab a baggie of apple slices that are beginning to brown. I put them on a plate, and I add one tablespoon of peanut butter from the cupboard just like the article in the magazine said to do for a healthy snack, not more and not less than one tablespoon.

Justine's still staring at the floor like she's had a spell put over her and she's frozen. Is she even blinking? I put my hand on her arm to snap her out of it. I feel bad for yelling at her, but this is getting out of hand.

"Why don't you go change and I'll take him this snack," I tell her.

I have no problem being the bad guy with Jojo.

She shrugs her shoulders and by the way she walks slowly to the bathroom, I sense that her heart is being shattered everyday with this rollercoaster of wanting to do the right thing but also wanting to love Jojo in any way she can.

Confident that I've set Justine straight, it's now time to have a talk with Jojo. We all need a reset. For the first time since I began this plan, the unfairness of it all is setting in. I grab the plate and make my way toward my brother's room. Ponyboy unexpectedly rushes under my feet, seeking revenge for dropping him earlier. This sudden movement causes me to falter, and the plate tips over, sending the apples rolling and tumbling onto the ground. Checking them for any stray cat hairs or carpet fuzz, I gather them up and restack them onto the plate while glaring at Pony, who seems unfazed and stares off indifferently, pretending he did nothing wrong as usual.

Jojo and Justine were already dating when he got hurt, so their relationship will stay intact if I go back in time. It seems that I stand to lose the most. I keep wondering if there's a way to prevent the situation from becoming the out-of-control mess it has without going all the way back to the night of the injury. I wouldn't be able to bring football back into his life, but I could try to keep him from becoming obese and lost. He's supposed to be in college right now, not trapped in his room with just a gaming console for company.

Maybe if I go back to a few months after I started dating Frankie, I can prevent Jojo from gaining the weight, which would make a huge difference. He'd still lose football but not his freedom, and I'd still have my relationship with Frankie. Thinking through all of this makes my stomach feel like it's trying to digest rocks. I feel even worse when I think about how fun it would be to relive things with Frankie again. I'm the asshole, not Justine.

CARRIE BEAMER

Chapter Five

The stifling air in Jojo's room hits me with all the force of an actual punch to the face, making me step backward for a second. I know it's not just me, because Pony turns around and trots back down the hallway. The aroma in his room is thick and draining with a mix of bad breath and stale air, and the only sliver of light is coming from the T.V. that my parents moved in here from the basement. His only form of entertainment is playing video games for hours, and he resembles a zombie with a distant look on his face.

I slide open his curtains like they were when I left his room this morning and he says, "Leave them, Des."

"How'd you know it was me?" He hasn't turned to see me yet.

"Because Justine smells like happiness, and you smell like torture," he says with his back to me still.

I sniff my arm for a second even though I realize torture doesn't have a smell—or does it? I'm pretty sure the smell of torture is this dank bedroom. "Sitting in the dark isn't going to help your mood today. This room needs some fresh air. This room needs a lot of things." I force the curtains all the way open and lift his window.

A warm spring breeze instantly rushes in, carrying with it the floral perfume of the lavender bushes my mom has planted out front. My mom planted five lavender bushes a couple of years ago and only one made it, but you can catch traces of lavender all over the house when the windows are open. My mom calls it nature's potpourri.

I shift my gaze to Jojo, and it's hard not to notice his massive physique that resembles a compact chest of drawers and not feel scared for him. His shirt hangs off him like a sagging mini parachute, and the skin on his visible arm is rough and flaky, like a parched pot of soil left baking in the sun for days. I can't help but cringe at the sight of his dry, itchy arm. I need to remember to bring him some lotion to soothe his skin. As I stand there, I feel uneasy, waiting for him to turn his head and acknowledge me. I let out a dramatic sigh, hoping to capture his attention.

He still doesn't look at me.

Fine, I'm going to ignore his pity party.

"Smell that? How can you resist the happiness the smell of mom's plants brings," I say, continuing to feel like a therapist that's trying to convince my patient that life isn't the tragedy he thinks it is even though his life has been a trashed mess since his football injury.

"Soak it in, Jo," I say, inhaling loudly.

He murmurs something that sounds like 'piss off' as he rolls to face me. This is my opportunity to move the plate of apples on the nightstand closer, so he knows the reason I'm in here and not Justine.

Ponyboy comes back and jumps up to sit in the windowsill and press his nose to the window screen, flipping his tail right to left. He's itching to get outside. I can't imagine the trouble the little maniac would cause if he was an outdoor cat.

I nod to myself, pleased that I've improved the vibe in here. Sunshine and fresh air are vastly underestimated when it comes to lifting a bad mood in my opinion. Seeing the scowl spread across my brother's face, I can tell he's not convinced, or he's seriously pissed his snack is apples—probably both.

My heart is heavy as I see him struggle to find comfort in his own body. It's as if every move causes him pain, and my own pain deepens as I watch him try to prop himself up against the wall. The memories flood back to me, of months after his injury when he could still sit with ease and chat with me and Justine before dinner. I can picture him now, sitting on his bed with a box of donuts on the floor, courtesy of the boxes Frankie used to bring my family every morning after work. He would absentmindedly stuff one donut after another into his mouth while Justine animatedly chatted beside him about friends or some upcoming school event.

At least after eating all that crap, he could leave his room and come down to join us for dinner at the table. I can still vividly recall how he would pile my mom's chicken and Spanish rice casserole onto his plate, and it was scary to see him eating so much after gorging himself on donuts minutes before. As he shoveled in bite after bite, he stared down at his plate without looking or engaging with any of us, as if he was oblivious to his surroundings. It was becoming clear that he was turning into a mere shadow of his former self since his injury, and I never could've predicted how severe his condition would become.

Now, he's just stuck. Stuck in this endless cycle of eating, sleeping, and playing video games or watching television in the evenings with Justine. The weights and exercise bands Frankie thoughtfully provided for him lay neglected on the floor like unwanted trash. It's as if they're a burden, a constant reminder of what he could no longer do. The vibrant colors of the bands and the shiny metal of the weights now seem dull and lifeless like garage sale items nobody wants, mirroring the way he feels inside.

"Hey," Justine says. She's standing in the doorway, her arms wrapped tightly around her stomach with her small button nose red from crying earlier. At least she changed into some sweats and a tank top. She looked truly jacked up in that *Carrie* costume. Frankie's right, I need to go easier on her. The girl has had a rough go at life. She lives alone with her alcoholic dad. Her mom left them when Justine was only five years old and never returned for her daughter. The thought of a parent abandoning their child, especially to be raised by someone who was fighting addiction with no resources to get better, is unimaginable. It's hard to understand how someone could walk away from their own flesh and blood without any consideration for their well-being and future. Justine and Rafa both got a raw deal when it came to family.

It wasn't until the night of Justine's sophomore year school choir concert that anyone knew how bad her home life was. According to Jojo, the choir was on the risers bellowing out the school's rendition of Bohemian Rhapsody, and her dad stumbled into the auditorium shouting the lyrics and causing chaos as he tripped over chairs and made a spectacle of himself. The other parents looked on in shock as Mr. James, the choir teacher, refused to halt the performance he'd worked so hard on all semester despite the obvious disruption caused by her drunken dad. It was a horrifying incident, and everyone began wondering about the sort of environment Justine was living in with him.

Justine ended up jumping off the risers mid-song—her face flamed with anger and humiliation—to usher him out. I can't imagine what her house is like. None of us have ever been inside, and she doesn't like to talk about her dad. I don't even know his name or her mom's name for that matter. I've never dared ask her for fear of stirring up pain I can't begin to comprehend.

Ever since Justine started attending the local community college, she practically never goes to her own house anymore. During the day, she attends classes while she's working toward becoming a nurse, and when she's not studying, she's working at our family's shop. Having lost most of her friends due to Jojo's condition, she now spends most of her free time sitting with him. Her former friends gave up on her, and she let them. Her only friends now are me and Frankie. Frankie wants to be a nurse too, so they at least have that in common.

"Hey," I say back, as she steps inside with that fragile, eyes turned down look of worry that lives on her face most days. To be honest, it always sort of has, it's just worse now.

As soon as Justine steps into the room, a broad smile spreads across Jojo's face, and he pats the bed next to him, gesturing for her to sit down. From the way his rich, chocolate-brown eyes light up in her presence, it's clear that she's the only one who can bring out a hint of the old Jojo. It's remarkable, especially considering that they haven't been on a real date in years, and I can't imagine there's any physical intimacy beyond kissing. He'd never let her witness the ravages of his once-athletic body in its current state.

"That's not macaroni and cheese," Jojo says, turning his attention to me. He points at the untouched apples that have been sniffed by the cat multiple times by now. He doesn't look at Justine or even blame her, because he knows I caused the change of plans he had for his snack today. Justine would never be blamed for anything anyway.

"Look, I added some peanut butter. It's really a delicious combination. Just try it, Jo." I bite my bottom lip, hoping something about the added nut butter helps my case.

Who am I kidding?

"No thanks," he says, shoving the plate so hard the apples almost slide off and fall to the ground for the second time today.

How dare he shove my snack away.

"Don't start, okay? We had a plan, and you're not sticking to your part of it. I'm doing everything I can to help you." Looking him directly in the eyes, I can see Justine in my peripheral vision tapping her leg up and down in a nervous jitter.

"No, you had a plan and just assumed I agreed because everyone else did," he says, holding my stare.

"Look, you guys, I think everyone is doing their best. Okay?" Justine says. She hates this conflict, and her attempt to diffuse my irritation isn't going to work. I'm sort of stunned she spoke up for the second time today. Maybe that *Carrie* costume empowered her to be a badass or something. Normally she'd curl into herself like a turtle ducking into its shell.

"Their best? You call cheesy pasta your best? You've got to be kidding me. Can you possibly be any more full of crap, Justine," I shout, not meaning to raise my voice. I just think what she's saying is ludicrous. Every amount of resistance I get from either of them feels like a personal attack on my life and what I stand to lose even if they don't know that.

"Don't you dare shout at her. Ever!" Jojo says. His chest heaves up and down as he tries reclaiming his breathing.

But I don't care how mad he is, I'm furious.

"Or what, Jojo? What are you going to do about it? Huh? Are you going to get up and chase me out of your room? No, you're not. You can't leave your room because all you do is eat crappy food day after day! And Justine is helping you stay trapped. Wake up, Jojo! You're dying in here! Thanks for nothing, Justine! Maybe everyone else can watch you do this to yourself, but I refuse!"

The room goes dead quiet save for the curtains

blowing and gently tapping on the window, and I know I've gone too far. I can see a visible pulse in my brother's neck he's so livid. Justine's staring at me with her mouth open and her eyes wide like a raccoon just caught digging through the trash by an angry homeowner holding a broom. With his hands balled into fists on his chest like an angry animal, Jojo looks like he wants to grab my throat and strangle me.

Lowering my voice to a whisper, I say, "Could you excuse me for one minute." I turn to run out of the room in an attempt to get outside and swing this moment away. In my desperation to get the hell out of here as fast as I can, I stub my toe on one of the hand weights lying on the floor and topple forward onto Justine.

"Whoa, are you…? What are you?"

She can't even finish her sentence. I somehow manage to slide off her lap and onto the floor like melted cheese sliding off of a piece of greasy pizza. She instantly pulls her knees up to her chest, ridding herself of the possibility that I might land on her again.

Crawling out of there, I only stand up when I get to the hallway. I speed walk the rest of the way through the house and out to the swing set. I swear my body used to function so much better before this whole time travel craziness.

I swing fast and furious, pumping my legs like my life depended on it, thinking of the moment right before Justine came into my brother's room. I barely notice the neighbor kids jumping on the trampoline next door. These kids never seem to feel the ground shaking when I swing, and it's bizarre. The ground rumbles and I feel like a balloon that was released into the sky after being tethered to a child's hand for way too long. Jumping off the seat, I reluctantly leave the backyard. I casually walk back into my brother's room with the plate of apples as if the fight we just had moments ago never happened—for him and Justine it didn't.

"Hey," Justine says from the doorway, looking just as sad as she did the first time this took place. I could've swung away, letting her have it in the kitchen, but I think that needed to happen.

"Hey," I say and with the spring breeze still blowing in the window, I start walking out of Jojo's room. I pause in his doorway, thinking about how to deliver the words I said before. I need to keep my tone serious but not attack him or Justine—that clearly won't get me anywhere.

"Even though you were expecting macaroni and cheese, it isn't on your food list. Justine made it for you, and I dumped it. Sorry, Jo, I just can't watch you continue killing yourself with food." Before anyone can say anything to me, I walk all the way out. He can eat the apples or not, but either way he's not getting the pasta. At least I didn't drop the plate of apples to the ground like the first go round.

Chapter Six

By the time I make Jojo's veggie stuffed turkey sandwich for dinner, I'm running late for my burger date with Frankie. It was the stupid strawberry hearts I made to liven up his plate that made me run behind. The lingering feelings of frustration and regret from his apple snack this afternoon made me do it. If someone brought me a plate with fruit that had been cut up into little hearts, it would definitely cheer me up, I decided. It's these things I do to help myself feel better about lording over my brother's meals. It's not lost on me that I'm going for a juicy burger while I shove veggies and turkey at my brother daily. At least I don't tell him I'm going for a burger, but I know he knows it's burger night. He used to be at burger night, too.

I leave the plate on the kitchen counter. Justine or my mom can take it up to him tonight. It saves me the drama of possibly arguing with him again when he rejects my perfectly planned plate.

Now I only have twenty minutes to freshen up my hair and makeup before Frankie gets here. I stop to take in my *Footloose* poster. Frankie and I saw it in the theatre a couple of weeks ago, and I was so captivated by Ren McCormack that Frankie bought me a poster to tease me. Jokes on Frankie because Kevin Bacon is now a permanent fixture on my wall.

Across my bedroom, I hear voices floating through my window from the driveway below. I turn my curling iron on and peer out to see my mom and dad standing on the driveway talking to Frankie, who's parked along the curb. Frankie's early which shouldn't surprise me. Why do couples always have an early person and a running late person? If not for Frankie, I'd never be on time for anything. And he'd never be late to school—I'm working on it.

My parents are dressed like Luke Skywalker and Princess Leia. My dad's bent over with his hands on his knees, laughing like he always does when my mom's telling a story. She never fails to crack my dad up—I think it's why he married her. Squinting, I can't tell if it's a wig or if my mom twisted her long black hair into the buns I see on each side of her head. She makes a pretty good Leia. Star Wars is a one of their favorites. I think they overdo it a bit wearing these costumes all the time, but who am I to judge their fun. They're one of a kind, that's for sure.

The mere thought of the delicious burgers Frankie and I are about to indulge in brings about a growling sensation in my stomach. My guilty conscience sets in again about Jojo's dinner. In my rush to get outside, I forgo the spirals I'd initially intended to add to my hair and settle for a quick brush-through. After switching off my curling iron, I take pride in the fact that my complexion has finally cleared up after years of struggling with blemishes. I've considerably reduced the amount of makeup I wear, limiting myself to just a thin layer of eyeliner, mascara, and a coat of Max Factor lipstick in the alluring shade of iced plum, carefully chosen by Rafa. While I have an urge to experiment with my makeup routine, I've grown dependent on Rafa's advice and hence, I stick to my trusted iced plum shade.

As I attempt to open the front storm door to greet Frankie and my parents on the driveway, it suddenly surges forward with great force, nearly slipping out of my grip. I release a yelp, yet somehow manage to retain my grasp on the door. I barely avoid a collision with my mother's empty terracotta flowerpots situated next to the porch swing we've had perched here as long as I can remember. As if on cue, the wind picks up again, causing me to exert significant effort to shut the front door.

My parents turn to look at me with their eyes crinkling against the blowing wind.

"You look nice," my mom says as I approach Frankie's jeep.

"Thanks. And may the force be with you," I say with a bow.

"We look pretty good, don't we?" my dad asks as he pushes his glasses back up the bridge of his nose like I haven't seen them dressed like this a million other times.

"Well, I'm not sure Luke Skywalker had that thick layer of black hair, Dad. You might consider trying the wig next time you wear this for a little more authenticity."

"Oh, he tried the wig again, but his hair is such a thick, bushy nest that it wouldn't fit. We tucked and tucked, but that mop on his head wouldn't budge. I don't think it would've stayed put in this wind anyway. Woweee, it's blowing out here." My mom laughs and ruffles Dad's fluffy hair that's whooshing around wildly.

We always joke that Dad at age forty-five, when most men have lost a good chunk of hair, could hide a small rodent in his full mop. It's barely even gray. It must be his Spanish Zaragozana mother that gave us all the thick, dark hair we have. I'm not complaining.

"Yeah, wigs were not made for me, that's for sure," Dad agrees.

"We better get going. We have burgers waiting for us at Pete's," I say, glancing up at Frankie, who has apparently been staring at me with a wide smile on his face this whole time.

"I left Jojo's dinner in the kitchen, unless Justine already took it to him."

They don't respond to that piece of information,

but I know they heard me.

I swallow down the knot in my throat, feeling so alone in my diet restrictions for my brother. I walk around to the passenger side of Frankie's jeep, and he leans over to open my door.

"Enjoy your pickles with a side of burger," my dad says, grinning.

"You know we will," Frankie says.

"Try not to be out past ten. The weatherman said on the news this morning that we have a pretty strong storm coming in tonight after dark." My mom looks up at the sky. Then she checks the bun on each side of her head to make sure they're still intact and sighs.

Missouri weather exhausts us all.

"Let's hope they're wrong. I don't want to replace the roof again. The last thing I need is for the roof to get more damage. That storm a few weeks ago was so bad I thought the walls were going to fly off the house," Dad says.

Struggling with the jeep door, I steal a quick glimpse at my surroundings, noticing that the sky bears an ominous appearance that hints at the impending storm. A wild idea strikes me. Maybe I can rescue Jojo from this nightmare without resorting to time travel after all. It's becoming more and more obvious to me that the changes I've tried to make with his diet have failed to cause any sort of positive outcome, physically or mentally. I can't persuade anyone at home to comply with the rules or help me with any of it. It's evident that I have to come up with a drastic plan, no matter how far-fetched it may seem. Anything, at this point, is worth a try, no matter how crazy the idea is.

Chapter Seven

Pete's outdoor seating area is brimming with a throng of people holding ice cream cones. They're generously topped with swirls of chocolate and vanilla soft serve stacked all the way to their eyeballs. To avoid the whole thing toppling onto the table or their clothes, they have to lick frantically. Cones that big are too stressful. I can't enjoy something I have to lick like a maniac, or it will start melting down my arm.

Everyone occupying the tables has resorted to using their elbows as weights to anchor down their napkins and burger wrappers. The whole scene just looks rushed and unenjoyable. I get that after a long Missouri winter they just want to be outside with the sun on their faces, that they crave fresh air and other people, but good grief give it up already. They act as if they're unaware that spring in Kansas City can be just as unpredictable and ridiculous as winter. From November to June, the weather can range from snow and ice to heavy rain and straight-line winds, making it difficult to enjoy being outside half of the time. Jojo's birthday is in March, and my mom tried planning an outdoor birthday party for him many years in a row. They always turned out to be a disaster thanks to the weather.

"Why would anyone try to eat outside in this wind?" I comment as Frankie parks the jeep next to a van full of kids who look like they just came from soccer practice. They're jumping around in back with red matching shirts on that say Candy's Cookie Factory. The back of the van even has a slight bounce to it with all the commotion. Too bad Candy doesn't own a candy factory I think to myself.

The woman situated in the front of the van averts

her attention toward the rowdy kid chaos going on behind her, shushing them in an attempt to gather her thoughts. Her high ponytail, which I'm guessing was once perfectly straight, now rests lopsided on her head, with stray strands of hair cascading down her face. Her cheeks are flushed from exerting her authority over her rambunctious crew who continue jumping around like popcorn kernels on a hot skillet. In that moment, she glances in my direction with an expression that only an utterly exhausted mother could wear. I offer a sympathetic smile as I take notice that she has five boys piled up in there.

"Some people like to have food blown all over their shirts I guess," he says, shaking his head, laughing as we both watch one man's condiment cup of ketchup blow right onto his lap.

The woman in the van unloads all the bobbing, blond boys, trying to corral them all into Pete's.

Frankie smiles. "I bet those kids give her a serious run for her money. Look at them. They look like they're having the time of their lives just walking in to get dinner," he says. "Lucky dogs."

He's right. Two of them are playfully hitting each other on the head, resulting in cackles of laughter, while another one is showing the smallest one of the group a rock he recently discovered in the parking lot. The two of them are huddled together, their faces beaming with excitement and wonder over their rare find, which is just a simple rock to the rest of us. There's only one in the group who dutifully grasps his mother's hand and looks back at the others, who seem to be acting like wild animals. He rolls his eyes and frowns at them, as if to express his disapproval, before quickly checking if his mother is watching him, as if to signal that they're in this together.

"That one right there," I say, pointing to the boy walking with his mom, "is the tattletale."

"Oh, come on, he's not a tattle, he just loves his mom," Frankie argues, grinning.

"Ha! He's for sure the goody-goody of the bunch. What a sucker he is for missing out on all the fun," I say.

Frankie smiles and squeezes my thigh, making me squirm in my seat, laughing.

"You're right. He can love his mom at bedtime, but right now he should be racing across this parking lot, raising hell with his brothers like he's supposed to."

Frankie stares after them with a look of wonder.

Frankie is an only child. The night we met I asked him if he had siblings since he knew Jojo, and he just shook his head no. He didn't act sad about it because he didn't know what he was missing. It's difficult for me to fathom what it would be like to grow up without a sibling like Jojo. Having a sibling gives you the emotional support necessary to carry the family's baggage, which can be a burden too heavy for one person to handle at times.

When you lose your childhood dog, your sibling is the only one that can truly empathize with the pain and sadness you feel. They knew that the dog was a significant responsibility, especially on Saturday mornings when he would bark incessantly to go outside and one of you had to drag yourself out of bed to let him out. But you all loved him despite the annoyance. They feel the same sense of loss and yearning for the wake-up call of licks and barks. Shared grief is somehow comforting.

When you fall from a tree that you weren't supposed to climb so you can test out the zipline one of the neighborhood boys made, your sibling is there to help you. They practically have to carry you home and help you hide the broken ribs you now have from your parents, so you don't get grounded for testing a rickety zipline you were told a million times not to ride. It was actually Jojo, showing his bravery to all the neighbor kids, who fell from the tree, not me. Even though you may argue and resent your sibling for their selfishness or for taking the last ice cream sandwich in the freezer, you cannot envision your life without them. I'm sad that Frankie doesn't have that and neither does Justine or Rafa for that matter. I suppose none of them really know what they're missing.

Once all the boys safely cross the parking lot and we're done people watching, we get out of the jeep and head toward our burgers. One of the reasons why I enjoy our Monday night burger routine, apart from the yummy burgers of course, is that I find listening to Frankie's stories a welcome escape from my life. Frankie has a knack for talking and can go on for an hour about anything and everything, which lets me lose myself in his hilarious chatter.

The enthusiasm he exudes when he recalls stories such as his parents recording themselves on their backyard trampoline, and subsequently replaying it while foolishly laughing at how his mother's boobs nearly knock her out during a jump, always strengthens my fondness for his family. Being with Frankie enables me to let go of all the anxieties that come with Jojo for a time, and I find solace in his presence.

"Hey, hottie hotness," Jake Brackston says to me as we walk in.

Pushing my hair, that was just blown all over my head outside, from my eyes, my happiness is immediately stolen by the mere presence of Jake. I forgot to prepare myself for this annoyance that never seems to go away.

I truly wish he didn't have to work on Monday

nights because he can be incredibly irritating and downright rude. For years now, every Monday night, he has persistently flirted with me right in front of Frankie, even when he himself has been in a relationship. Luckily, he attends the private school located in our town, so I'm spared from having to deal with him during the day. I feel sorry for the girls who do attend his school. I bet he drives them all batty.

"Hey, Jake," Frankie says, sliding the hand not holding mine into his pocket. "We'll take our usual. Don't forget the extra pickles. You guys have been going a little light lately." He smiles at Jake and then at me.

"I would never forget Dessy's pickles. I don't want to disappoint her hotness," he says, flashing me a huge, wide-mouthed grin that I return with a scowl.

"Suck it, Jake."

"Thanks, man. I appreciate you keeping my girl happy." Frankie plants a kiss on my cheek and gives Jake another smile.

Jake's eyebrows pinch together as he looks at Frankie with a bewildered expression on his face. He's frustrated by the fact that I don't pay him any attention and that Frankie isn't bothered one bit by his gross behavior. Frankie's aware that he doesn't need to pay any heed to the brazen ogling of this self-assured twit. Since the day Frankie and I shared a kiss after a football game cementing our relationship, I've only had eyes for him, and he understands this because he feels the same way about me. There's no greater feeling than being loved as much as you love someone.

Jake's physical attractiveness becomes inconsequential once he speaks. When Rafa and I used to come in here after school so that Rafa could satisfy his craving for onion rings, which was also an excuse to check out all the cuties who came in, Jake would constantly ask me out. This was before my relationship with Frankie, so I'm confused as to why he would assume I'd be flattered by his obnoxious flirting now, when I wouldn't give him the time of day before. Rafa always referred to him as "Jake the gigolo".

Jake wordlessly hands our drinks to Frankie, but he quickly winks at me in the hopes of gaining something—I don't know what—from me before spinning on his heels to grab our fries and burgers. He's aware that he won't even get a smirk from me today or ever for that matter, but he won't stop his flirtatious behavior the next time we visit. It's an endless cycle of annoyance. Frankie hands me my Dr. Pepper, and I take a pull from my straw, yearning for the spicy kick of the carbonation hitting my throat before tickling my nose. There's something about Pete's syrup-to-carbonation ratio and the chewy pellet ice that makes this the best soda in town. Frankie slides our tray of food off the counter and leads me to our booth in the back.

"We lucked out tonight," Frankie says when he sees that our favorite booth in the back along the front window is open.

I scoot in across from him, feeling energized about my new plan. The hope of something better for Jojo. "So, I need your help with something. Would your dad let me borrow any of his tools? You know my dad has nothing besides maybe a screwdriver in our unorganized mess of a garage."

"Why?" he asks, drawing the word out in a puzzled question.

"Because he's the least handy person on the planet, you know that," I say, peeling a warm pickle drenched in ketchup from my burger and popping it into my mouth.

"No, I mean why do *you* need tools?"

"Oh, right. I need some sort of saw and a hammer mostly, I think," I say, not exactly answering his question.

The mere thought about what I want to do is now making me sweat, and I can feel the backs of my legs sticking to the fake leather of the booth seat like gum stuck on a warm sidewalk. Frankie's dad owns a pool construction company called Rubio Construction, and their garage is like a Home Depot. The whole garage is a treasure trove of tools and supplies. Just like Home Depot, every item is neatly arranged, with clear labeling and storage hooks and bins. It's impressive, but he's very controlling about anyone borrowing his tools, so this is asking a lot of Frankie.

For a second, he frowns in confusion and concern setting his burger down. "What exactly are you planning to do?"

Clearly the thought of me using a saw has him worried, as it should. Me using a saw would be a very unwise decision, especially with Ponyboy in the house. I'd probably lose a finger or two.

"Well ... I was hoping you could handle the construction aspect of this new plan, while I provide emotional support? I wouldn't be the one handling the tools, I'm not crazy. Also, it has to be done when my parents aren't home because they might kill us." I lift one eyebrow and wait for him to respond. Overwhelmed with anxiety, I slide to the corner of the booth and hold my breath. If he says he won't be able to help me, I'll be left in the same predicament as before.

"Dessy, just tell me what you're talking about. You know I'm always here to help you with anything." He massages the back of his neck, nervously awaiting my reply.

Blowing out all the air I was just holding, I blurt

out, "I want to cut Jojo's doorway out. We just have to remove some of the surrounding wall." I slap my hand over my mouth to refrain from saying anything more that could make this idea sound more nuts than it already does and wait for his reaction.

Now he backs into the corner on his side of the booth and puts one knee up. We sit in silence for a minute, both of us thinking.

"Mr. Strand next door widened his doorways when his wife needed to use a walker after her stroke. My dad said it cost him a fortune, but I think we could do one doorway ourselves. Yes? Your dad has the tools to do this, right?"

"Whoa, that's major." Now he lets out an uneasy breath.

"I really think that if he can break free from the gloom and doom of his room and experience life again, he'll be motivated to stick to his diet. I mean initially the transition may be a challenge with his bad leg but I'm confident he'll overcome it all once he's out and about. He can even go back to physical therapy for his leg!" I exclaim, almost shouting. Embarrassed by my outburst, I cover my mouth again. This is all I've got right now, and I need it to work.

He takes a bite of his burger and hesitates to debate on what this will really entail.

"I have to examine the wall to determine if it's possible to cut it out. You can't cut out just any wall in a house," he explains, pondering while gazing at the ceiling. "Did your parents ever mention removing him from his room like this?"

"In my house, there's a collective denial about Jojo's condition improving over time and the issue resolving on its own. Even though we all know when Jojo tries to leave his room and he can't even fit through the doorway, it's a devastating blow to his mental state, no one is willing to take a bold step." I say, finishing off every last pickle on my burger. I don't know why I eat them before I eat my burger, but I just love how warm and tangy they taste peeled from the bun.

Frankie works with his dad during the summer, and he knows about construction. His dad isn't thrilled that he's wanting to be a nurse instead of help run the family business, but I'm glad he's going to do what will make him happy. He'll make a wonderful nurse with all the compassion he has for people. I think Justine and Frankie would make a hell of a nursing team. What with his compassion and her ability to push through any tragedy and put others first. I could never be a nurse. It's the whole touching a stranger thing I couldn't get past. And forget it if they're bleeding. I'm out on blood. The sight of blood makes me see spots, and I get dizzy and puke.

"Okay, yeah, so will you at least look at it and tell me what you think we can do without messing something major up? I'm not trying to collapse our roof or anything. The weather around here is hard enough on it."

"Well, no matter what, we're definitely going to mess something up. I just want to make sure we don't cause the kind of major damage you're referring to." He moves forward and looks me right in the eyes just like the first night I met him. My heart flutters a bit at his intense gaze. God, I love him. "You're positive this is what you want to do? I mean you've obviously thought this through."

"Actually, I only just thought of it tonight." I feel the start of tears coming. "I think this can really work though, and I'm hoping when my parents see the change it makes in Jojo, they won't be so pissed that I, well you, cut a hole in their wall. It's time for something that will wake the whole family up."

He nods and takes my hand from across the table. "Then I'll do it on one condition."

"Anything," I say, already feeling the emotion in my throat that he's willing to do this for me. I've made him deal with so much concerning my brother, and he never makes me feel guilty about making him share in this burden.

"Promise me that you won't even think about touching any of the tools I bring over," he says, being more serious about that than cutting the hole.

I exhale and get up to go sit next to him. Falling in beside him, I wrap my arms around his neck and kiss his cheek. I pull back to look at him. "You couldn't pay me to touch a saw. I'd like to keep all these, thank you very much." I hold my hands up and waggle my fingers in his face.

"Then you have yourself a deal, but God help us," he says, laughing uneasily.

Frankie's agreement ignites a blazing determination inside me, spurring me toward a new plan. My stomach flips with anticipation, even though I'm trembling with fear just thinking about it. I'm filled with a newfound sense of hope I haven't felt in what seems like an eternity. I push aside the doubts and try not to dwell on the endless possibilities of things going wrong. I can always swing it away.

Chapter Eight

We sit in silence for a moment, side by side, each lost in our own thoughts and enjoying the rest of our dinner. The sound of searing burgers and the chitchat of other diners fill the air as people and families come and go, finishing their day with an ice cream sundae or bag of curly fries. It is a rare uncomplicated moment that I wanted to enjoy before going back home.

Frankie leans forward, resting his elbows on the table before turning to me. "How do you think your mom and dad will react once we do this? Will they ban me from the house forever?" He smiles, but I can tell he's worried they'll be angry with him. To be honest, I know he wants the heat off of me for this, but I won't let it happen.

Thinking about the impending changes we're going to make, I let out a small, nervous laugh. "My dad will handle the situation by pretending as if nothing has changed, while my mom will completely flip her lid. She won't flip on you—she'll know I orchestrated the whole mess. But maybe if they'd helped me more with Jojo's diet, I wouldn't have resorted to this. The wood being altered is what will send my mom over the edge."

It's no secret my mom holds a deep attachment to the intricate carvings of the woodwork of our house, which was a significant factor in her reluctance to widen the doorways when Mr. Strand next door suggested his contractor to us. The wood is a deep, rich mahogany color, which contrasts beautifully with the lighter hues of the surrounding walls. The design is refined, with smooth curves and sharp angles that work together to create a sense of depth and texture. The intricate patterns and motifs seem to tell a story, as if each carving has its own tale to share. The woodwork extends from the frame to the door itself, which is equally gorgeous.

My dad, on the other hand, could care less with matters of décor. If my mom is happy, he's good with whatever. I love that about him. I can't ignore the nagging feeling that as soon as my mom sees the change to the precious wood, there will be no containing her outrage.

"As soon as the hole's cut, you can run away and hide from my family forever if you want. But it'll blow over hopefully once Jojo is up and out of there. My brother walking out of his room should shut down all the anger thrown your way."

"I'll try to see what I can do about saving the woodwork the best I can, but you better believe as soon as I'm done cutting, I'll be packing up my tools and running out of there faster than the Mighty Dogger has ever moved. I can't believe I've agreed to this."

This makes us both laugh, but we can feel the tension hanging over our heads like a dark cloud ready to unleash a hailstorm.

Observing a lady's impressive ability to balance two drinks and lay a napkin down without it being carried away by the wind outside, I say, "It looks like the wind has died down."

Casting a quick glance toward the parking lot, we notice that everything has become eerily calm. The once-bending trees are now barely in motion, and even the scattered food wrappers previously whirling around aimlessly seem to have a newfound stillness. I have no doubt Frankie will want to clean them up before we leave. He hates to see litter.

"This calm now means we're in for a crazy, house rattling storm tonight. The weather might take care of getting Jojo out of his room before we do," he says, packing up the empty food containers on our table.

"It also means we can go for our walk," I say, happy we don't have to go back to my house yet. My house has become a den of depression for all of us since Jojo was injured. It's swallowing everyone's happiness, but nobody seems to want to fix it. We don't know how.

"I was thinking the same thing," he says, motioning for me to get out of the booth. "Maybe we should grab some of the loose wrappers still lying about out there before we go." He motions to the litter outside.

I knew it.

"Of course." I smile and take his hand.

It is a perfect time to walk through a neighborhood we haven't explored yet. As the sun sinks behind the horizon, painting the sky with a warm palette of pink and orange, the once-windy night becomes cool and peaceful. We drive fifteen minutes away this time to find one we think looked interesting. Frankie parks and as we get out, I instantly feel dreamy, like nothing in the whole world can upset me. This is much needed tonight. Walking alone with Frankie is like being wrapped in a soft, fuzzy robe on a cold night, curled up with everyone you love.

Back when Frankie and I were just friends, we found ourselves in an unspoken dilemma of sorts, because we weren't sure if the other wanted to move our relationship beyond being just friends. We didn't want to mess up what we had going, so we decided to come up with activities that would not appear to be typical "boyfriend-girlfriend" outings, even though taking walks together was a total relationship thing to do. We ended up learning more about each other than we ever would've if we'd gone on the typical dates like parties or the movies our high school friends partook in. We were in no rush to take things to the next level because we both knew deep down that we were meant to be together.

We've never had any drama or issues—it's just that easy.

As we take our leisurely walks, we like to observe and discover specific yards that capture our attention with their abundance of blooming flowers or houses whose wacky paint colors and playful front doors stand out. I love the smells a neighborhood can have like the sweet scent of laundry detergent flowing from a nearby vent or a charcoal grill being fired up on someone's patio. These glimpses of family life always bring a smile to my face.

Frankie's favorite thing to do is gaze at the people behind the windows, observing their interactions, showing us a fleeting yet satisfying look into the lives of people we'll probably never meet but somehow find comfort in their domestic rituals. It sounds creepy, I know, but it's not. We don't linger in front of a house or anything like burglars casing the place.

We briefly pause and admire the warm glow of kitchen lights and the bustling movements of dinnertime routines. A mother meticulously folding the laundered clothes of her family while she's engrossed in a TV show is a common thing we see on weeknight evenings. Seeing someone laboring over the stove while a spouse is perched on a barstool engaged in lively conversation warms my heart for some reason. There's something soothing about seeing other people live their lives in a normal manner while walking with the love of your life as you imagine what your future holds together someday. It fills my spirit with enough goodness to trudge through my last year of high school without Rafa.

"Okay, so we've walked the whole street. Which one is your pick?" he asks me.

"I think it's a tie between the house with the purple flowers climbing up the white trellis or the one that had the porch swing and the lit-up lanterns on the front steps. You have to admit they were both equally beautiful, but you know I'm a sucker for a purple flower. Which one did you like?"

"Hmm, I think I liked the tan one we saw at the very beginning," he says, leading me back the way we came. It's fun to pass all the houses again on the way back to his jeep. Sometimes, we even change which house was our favorite on the second trip.

"The plain brownish one that has the creepy kidnapper van on the driveway and the cute as hell but loud barking beagle in the yard?"

"Yep, that's the one. That beagle was just saying hello, very loudly. But the van does look a bit creepy though," he says, nodding in agreement.

Work vans always seem creepy to kids.

"Why on Earth would you like that house out of all the unique ones we just saw?" I have to stop and look at him because that house was the only one on the block that seemed like it didn't belong with the others.

"You saw the van, but I saw the two kids in the upstairs window hanging upside down on their bunkbeds. I couldn't hear them screaming and squealing—thanks to the rambunctious beagle—but I could tell that's exactly what was going on just by the pure joy on their faces and their mouths open wide. They were having the best time on this random Monday night," he says, leaning in to kiss me.

How could I ever let go of a guy who has a heart like Frankie? My mood sinks as I let him wrap me into his arms, because even though I've found a solution to getting Jojo out of his room, I have a terrible feeling it won't work. It'll be up to Jojo to do the work once he's out of his room, and I'm not sure he has it in him anymore. He has lost his spark. It's something that can't be replaced like a doorframe, but it's all I can hope for.

I once again ignore the fact that I can just go back and fix it all for Jojo with a couple swings. I can't lose Frankie.

Chapter Nine

In my living room, perched atop a kitchen chair, adorned in a blue and white dress reminiscent of Dorothy's dress from "The Wizard of Oz", Justine waits patiently while my mom hems the dress's frayed hemline. Even with its well-worn appearance, the dress is a popular rental from my mom's shop, with the shop situated so close to the Kansas state line. My eyes travel from the dress back up to Justine, and I can't help but feel that she doesn't quite embody the bubbly charm of the iconic character of Dorothy. Justine lost her zeal and enthusiasm a while back—I can almost pinpoint the exact month. She needs this change to happen for Jojo just as much as the rest of us.

"Hey, how was Pete's?" my mom asks, mumbling around the pins she's holding in her mouth.

"It was good, as usual. That's a fitting costume for the weather I think we have coming tonight." I try not to look at Justine, who is sucked into a rerun of Dynasty. Justine hasn't even acknowledged me. She gets the same zombie look on her face my brother does when he's zoned out on video games.

My mom and Justine always have a show going, and I'm glad Justine has my mom to hang out with. She can only chill with Jojo for so long before I'm sure it gets boring as hell. How much can you sit in someone's room without losing your mind? Justine and Jojo are left with little choice but to spend their time together doing basically nothing. Sure, playing Donkey Kong can be fun, but it's hardly a substitute for the type of things they did before he was hurt. Those two went to every high school party there was. Her Friday nights have drastically changed, but I get the feeling she likes having a quiet night in with my family instead of all the high school drama.

I need to do more with Justine. Since Rafa moved away, I haven't really hung out with anyone aside from Frankie. I feel like Justine and I—despite my best efforts—won't ever connect the way I did with Rafa. Our relationship seems to have the tendency to take on a sisterly type of bond, which is further complicated by Jojo's situation.

I miss my Friday nights and after school hang outs with Rafa, but he isn't coming back to Missouri, and I don't blame him. His life is on the west coast now and he's happy. The harsh reality is that he's gone, and the financial burden of attending an out-of-state college close to him is simply not in my budget. Actually, I don't have a college budget, but I want to try to graduate from college with debt I can manage to pay off right before I die, not debt I'd take to my grave, like I would from a California school.

Rafa and I were loners. We only hung out with each other. Once I met Frankie, the two of them was all I needed. I've been hesitant to form any new friendships at school because I don't see the point when I'm going to be leaving for college in just five months. Frankie and I plan to attend Northwest Missouri State together, so why would I connect with anyone this late in the game? Instead, I've adopted a wait-and-see approach, hoping I meet some new friends once I get to college. This could of course all go to hell if I have to go back to the night Jojo got hurt. Going back would give me four more years until I can go to college—I'd have to go back to my freshman year. That seems crazy to me, absolutely nuts.

I refocus my thoughts because the possibility of redoing three years of high school makes me want to throw up.

GOING BACK FOR JOJO

"I have homework so..." I walk out of the living room like I'm not in a hurry to formulate a plan to destroy the drywall and my mom's favorite wood in the house. I'm dying to get a look at the doorway to my brother's room now that I know it's getting widened.

As I approach Jojo's room, I notice a faint glow emanating from underneath his door, signaling that he's watching TV. I take a step back to avoid casting a shadow he might see under the door and cautiously inspect his doorway. Upon closer inspection, I realize that cutting into either side of the wall could potentially jeopardize the stability of the ceiling above, just as Frankie had warned me. I'll have to wait until Frankie can get over here and look at it to know for sure.

I step over Ponyboy's sprawled out body on my bedroom floor and collapse onto my bed, mentally drained, my gaze fixated on the wall that separates my room from Jojo's. I'm worried about the impact doing this might have on my brother's fragile emotional state. Could this renovation be the change we desperately need, or will it only serve to sink him into deeper despair? He won't want to leave the house, but it'll surely help his mood to be at the dinner table with us again or sit on the couch and watch shows with my dad.

I hear Justine entering Jojo's room, closing the door behind her. Once Frankie's saw gets to work, the comfort of being behind closed doors will no longer be a luxury they can enjoy.

Sensing my anxiety, Ponyboy snuggles up in my lap, demonstrating a rare display of affection.

I shake off my doubt. I have little choice but to go ahead with operation "cut Jojo out". I take a bit of comfort in the fact that in the event of any major problems, I'll just go outside and swing the disaster away. I laugh to myself because of course it's going to be a major problem, but so is being trapped in your room and that's not funny—it's devastating.

****

The next day after school, I stand with Frankie while my brother's door looms in front of us, his dad's tools scattered at our feet. Frankie, with his keen eye and steady hand, examines the door, calculating the precise location where we need to cut.

I see the determination in his eyes as he weighs the risks and considers the potential consequences. Finally, with a nod of his head, he says it will be risky, but it can be done. He doesn't say it with confidence though.

Sweat gathers on his forehead with every second we wait to get started. He inhales deeply and picks up his dad's saw. "There's no going back once I start," he says with his construction goggles strapped on like a guy on a mission.

He'd feel better about this if he knew I could return it back to normal if he really screws this up. Justine and Jojo are in his room, and they have no idea what's about to happen. Frankie and I went back and forth on the drive over here about telling Justine, but we know she wouldn't have any useful input to this utterly crazy decision. She feeds him candy and soda for crap's sake.

"Okay, I'm ready," I say, shaking my hands out as if I'm doing anything besides watching. They've been clammy since we got all the tools picked up from Frankie's garage.

"Are you sure you don't want to warn them?" Frankie whispers, tapping his right foot nervously and pointing at Jojo's door.

"I'm sure. Just do it. My parents will be home in an hour, so get to it."

"Back up. I don't want you anywhere near this

saw, especially if your cat is roaming around here someplace. Just go sit on the floor and don't get up for any reason? Got it?" He points me toward the very end of the hall.

Backing slowly down the hall, I sit down, crossing my legs anxiously.

Frankie looks back at me, and I give him a firm nod. He turns toward the doorway, starting up some sort of cutting device.

To my surprise, the machine's deafening roar is even louder than I'd anticipated. It's a shock to hear such a loud power tool in my tiny hallway. As Frankie lifts one leg, a little off balance, and forcefully kicks a massive hole into the wall beside my brother's door, a wave of terror washes over me, causing me to instinctively cover my mouth with my hands. It takes all my emotional strength to restrain myself from impulsively abandoning the entire project and swinging it away before it has even begun. While Frankie proceeds cutting into the wall from the point of impact, Justine suddenly opens the door, revealing a look of utter astonishment on her face. Her mouth is open so wide in disbelief that I'm betting Frankie can see her back molars.

"What in the hell are you doing!" she screams over the roar blasting through the house. I've literally never heard her raise her voice, and it startles me as much as the saw did.

Ponyboy comes flying out of my brother's room with his eyes bulging, landing in my lap.

I bury my face in his fur and pretend Justine isn't screaming while Frankie keeps at it.

She's shouting question after question while she steps back farther into Jojo's room. I think she realizes Frankie isn't going to stop and she needs to get the hell out of the way. He doesn't have time to pause and talk this through with anyone, let alone Justine.

He briefly looks back at me, and I peek out from behind Ponyboy's fluffy back and give him a thumbs up. I think my parents might kill me, and I begin to panic. Sitting hunched over, trembling, taking deep, slow breaths to calm my nerves while waiting for Frankie to get done, I'm not prepared for what transpires next.

Suddenly, I spring to my feet as Frankie switches off the saw and releases it, allowing it to drop to the ground with a resounding thud that startles Pony, causing him to scurry loose from my arms and race down the hallway.

I think Ponyboy is done with us all for the day.

Chapter Ten

Frankie and I stand in motionless silence as a cloud of drywall and dust particles float through the air like ash raining down from a burning building. My brother stands in the doorway, panting heavily as though he has just done one of my mom's hour-long aerobic videos that seem to be collecting dust in our living room. With a firm grip on either side of the doorframe, Jojo tries desperately to steady himself.

Frankie hasn't yet cut out the frame, leaving only a colossal hole in the wall next to it, but at least the wood on the doorframe hasn't been touched yet.

"What the actual shit," I manage to whisper to no one in particular.

Frankie slowly bends down to pick up his tools and moves away from Jojo without taking his eyes off him like my brother is holding him at gunpoint. Then in a moment of pure social confusion, Frankie stands up straight and casually says, "Oh, hey, Jo, how's it going?"

Jojo struggles to catch his breath as he forces himself through the doorway, his body contorting as he tries to squeeze past the narrowness of the frame. One half of him remains inside the room with Justine—I'm assuming she's still in there and she didn't jump out the window to save herself—while the other half is slowly emerging through the door, as if he were being birthed from his own bedroom.

Frankie leans into me and gives me a quick kiss before darting down the hall. He yells a quick, "See you guys later."

I hear the front door slam shut. If I was Frankie, I would've run for my life too.

I watch in delight and horror as Jojo finally

manages to free himself from the dungeon that has held him down for more than a year.

"Oh my god, yes! Jojo, you're free!" I jump up and down in elation and start yelling for Justine to get out here with us. My brother is standing on two legs, and he's in the hall.

Justine peeks out from behind him but doesn't come out.

"Free?" he huffs.

Jojo's rage is making me hyperventilate again. Sweat begins pooling under my bra. "Uh, yeah. You're out of there," I say, pointing back at the room.

"I wasn't trapped, you idiot." He grimaces in pain and tries shifting his weight from one leg to the other.

"You mean to tell me you knew you could leave your room this whole time?" I feel my face reddening in anger and confusion.

"I do come out of my room. I just do it when I'm home alone or sometimes when everyone's asleep." He says this and gives an immediate but brief look at the ground in shame.

"Why the hell would you not come out and be with us?"

I stare at him, and he turns slightly like he might go back in his room.

"You just sit in there and make us all feel terrible for you! You don't even care what this is doing to Mom and Dad, not to mention Justine being stuck in there with you constantly!"

Justine looks at the ground, pretending she's invisible, and slumps back into the bedroom.

"Why would you just sit in there? Don't you want to get back to your life?"

This time he does turn away from me to head back to the safety of Justine and his dungeon.

I open my mouth to speak, but I'm interrupted by a scream coming from behind me that I haven't heard for ten years. I'm immediately taken right back to the time my brother choked on a Gobstopper when we were kids. The memory of my dad frantically performing the Heimlich maneuver while my mother ran in circles, her panicked screams piercing the air, flooded my thoughts for a second. I can still see the image of the yellow Gobstopper flying out of my brother's mouth and sticking in the brown carpet on our living room floor, while my mother broke down in tears. It was a traumatic event that has clearly stayed with me all this time.

We were never allowed hard candy again. I'm seventeen and if my mom caught me with hard candy to this day, she would slap it out of my hand. She once caught Justine opening a Jolly Rancher and took it right from her as Justine was attempting to put it in her mouth. With a slight shudder of her shoulders, she tossed it into the trash.

My dad rushes to the top of the stairs, alarmed by my mother's frantic screams. He probably fears that we may be experiencing another choking incident with the way she's losing it at the moment.

"Oh my God," my dad says, grabbing my mom's free hand that isn't gripped at her chest.

"Jojo, you're up," my mom says, dropping my dad's hand and moving toward us.

Jojo's still breathing heavy, as if it takes everything out of him to hold himself upright. Between breaths, he says, "Can everyone calm down? I can walk. What the hell did you think, I was just stuck?" He's not facing any of us.

"Well, yeah, that's exactly what we thought. You know that's what we thought, Jo," my mom says, confused. I can tell she's a little irritated at his attempt to act like this is no big deal. The more he acts like nothing new is happening, the crazier it makes me feel.

Jojo's eye rolling suggests he thinks we're all foolish idiots, even though he's the one who's kept his ability to leave his room concealed. Surely, Justine had no idea and must be just as upset as we are, but of course she'd never say that.

I begin wondering when someone will bring up the gaping hole in the wall and the debris of drywall scattered throughout the house. Making the decision to change all of this, I scoot past my parents down the hall, slip into the kitchen in my socks, and crash into a chair, knocking over my mom's Star Wars salt and pepper shakers. Then, I hastily make my way to the back porch, flinging myself onto the swing to escape the chaos. This is an utter disaster and now that I know Jojo can get up and out, things are going to change. I'm going back to seventh hour at school.

****

When Frankie and I leave school, I tell him that I've waited all day to tell him I heard Jojo get up in the middle of the night and actually leave his room. I told him how I peeked out of my bedroom and there was Jojo moving as quietly and as cautiously as he could. Of course, this isn't true, but I know this is exactly what my brother is doing thanks to Frankie cutting a hole in the wall that he'll never remember cutting. The first time around, Frankie and I were heading to get his dad's tools, but now Frankie's in stunned silence driving us to my house.

"Why does he wait until you guys are asleep?" he asks, still shaking his head in disbelief.

It feels odd to keep Frankie in the dark about what's truly going on. I want so badly to reveal my power to him, but I'm scared that doing so could violate some strange ass, outlandish rule like something from The Goonies, leading to unforeseen and bizarre consequences. I'm so desperate to blab the truth that I have to practice tremendous willpower to refrain from saying anything at all, for the sake of humanity. I typically share everything with Frankie, and this is making me nuts on top of everything else. I haven't even called Rafa to fill him in on any of this, which is honestly even more difficult.

"Why didn't you tell me this before school?" He's staring at the road ahead with an unfocused, vacant look of shock on his face at my new revelation.

Well, because I didn't know this before school. I didn't plan this very well.

"Oh, I wasn't sure if it was, I don't know, wrong to tell because Jojo clearly wants to hide it," I say, struggling to come up with something that will make sense. I clearly fail.

I hate it when this kind of thing happens. I should've just started the whole day over, but I'm glad I didn't. My college algebra class from today almost caused me a meltdown. I'm so over math. I want to major in journalism—I don't need algebra for that.

He tilts his head and looks sideways at me like something isn't adding up. He knows I would've called and woken him up in the middle of the night if I saw Jojo walking.

I try steering the conversation in a different direction. "So, what do I do? How do I confront him and tell him that I know that he's been pretending to be stuck? I've been waiting on him hand and foot for months, and I want answers. I'm not going to just keep acting like he's helpless. He needs to get up and get some help for his leg and all the weight that's making him miserable. Enough is enough."

Now that I think about all the meals I've made

him and the laundry I've done, I'm pissed. I know I chose to do these things, but he let me believe he couldn't.

"Why would he just let us all do everything for him? I don't get it," I say.

Frankie shifts in his seat, and I can tell he's still taking it all in. "He's depressed," he finally says. "What he needs is therapy. My mom works with several reliable therapist who can see him. I know she'd totally want to help. She can even find someone that will come to your house. They visit hospitals, so I'm sure they'd do therapy in a home for someone in his situation. I don't know why it never crossed my mind before. I guess I just assumed Jojo wouldn't be receptive to the idea."

Frankie's mom happens to be a therapist, but I tend to avoid discussing Jojo when I'm around his parents. It's not a topic I'm comfortable with and they're respectful of my boundaries, which is one of the reasons why I appreciate them so much.

"He won't be open to it, but now he's not going to have a choice. My parents and Justine need to get on board with helping convince him to talk to someone about it."

This reminds me that my parents don't know Jojo can leave his room, and I need to figure out how to tell them without it seeming odd that I know. I need to catch Jojo out of his room.

"Are you cool with me asking my mom for help?"

I appreciate how respectful Frankie is of my family's privacy where Jojo's concerned. He wants to help with this just as much as I do, and he doesn't even know what's at stake.

"That would really mean a lot to me," I say and lean over to kiss him.

He nods and intertwines our fingers, knowing this is a lot to handle.

GOING BACK FOR JOJO

After Frankie drops me off, instead of following my normal after-school routine of preparing a snack for Jojo and planning his dinner, I head straight to my room to finish my homework and wait. It's a good feeling to know that he can go to the kitchen if he wants to. I refuse to cater to his needs this time. When Jojo eventually gets hungry, he'll have to prepare something for himself or ask my parents. This night is going to be a game-changer for my family, and I no longer feel the need to go back in time now that I have a new plan.

At least I think I do.

CARRIE BEAMER

Chapter Eleven

I know I asked Frankie to see if his mom could help, but I decide what Jojo needs is more of a life coach. Jojo isn't going to reach any goals by talking to a therapist. Instead, he needs someone who can assist him in identifying his next steps to move forward, rather than focusing on his past losses.

I stumble across some potential life coaches in the Yellow Pages after noticing an advertisement in a magazine—which is where I got the idea. Before that, I had no idea these people existed. In my opinion, life coaching may be exactly what my brother needs to reclaim his life.

Judy Shewy, a local woman, catches my attention. Her name has a certain rhymey charm to it I can't resist.

Her answering machine message is overflowing with enthusiasm and warmth. I know right away she's the kind of person who will be able to help. I can't afford to waste any time, so I pour my heart out in a detailed message about Jojo's situation. And then, to my relief, she calls me back right away.

She tells me Jojo's situation appears to be a textbook example of self-medication. According to her, Jojo is using food to stifle the negative emotions he has due to his football injury. She believes Jojo has solely defined himself as a football player, and the inability to continue playing has left him feeling utterly lost. She assures me she knows just how to handle this, and we set up a time for her to come tomorrow at 4 PM sharp. I am surprised it is happening so fast. I don't have time to weigh the consequences—that is probably a good thing.

With that settled, I feel relief knowing help is on the way. Although her solution sounds credible, she didn't mention what she charges, and I'm hoping it won't be a crazy fee. I literally have no clue, nor can I guess what a life coach charges for a session. Sometimes my parents pay me when I work at the store, but that's very rare. I can't protest much since the shop provides me with food and a roof over my head, but it would be great to have some pocket money just in case you have a brother that needs a life coach. How is this my reality right now?

The floor outside Jojo's room creaks as Justine makes her way in and I can hear them talking in hushed voices. It isn't long before I hear the hum of the microwave emerging from the kitchen. When I never brought him a snack, or dinner for that matter, he didn't summon me at all—he never did before either I suppose. He has likely solicited Justine's help to fetch him something to eat. I should've known he would have Justine make him something—and something not on the approved meal list I gave my family. I'm sure she's presently concocting some sort of bready, greasy goodness. Was he always waiting for me to just give up and stop making healthy food for him? Was my whole family waiting with him?

****

I insist that Frankie stays with me after school. I'm worried about how Judy Shewy's visit will go, and my anxiety is skyrocketing. Fortunately, Justine is working at the shop today, which is a relief. The last thing I want to deal with is her emotional baggage on top of the overstuffed bags my brother's carrying or not carrying at the moment.

This morning, before Justine headed off to her classes, she took it upon herself to whip up a batch of pancakes for my brother. The warm, sweet, and inviting smell of the pancakes as the batter hit the hot pan in the kitchen released a rich, buttery aroma that filled our entire house. I love pancakes too, but the very thought of how all the work I've put in the last couple of months was being erased by these meals every day is maddening. I keep reminding myself that things will improve once Judy arrives to sprinkle her life coaching magic around like the cure Jojo needs.

As Justine makes her way through the hallway, holding a plate piled high with the sweet, syrup-drenched pancakes, the sheer look of terror and apprehension on her face when she has to pass me makes me feel a little better that she knows what she's doing is wrong. I even catch myself secretly hoping Pony will trip her up, but he's too busy ignoring our existence altogether. I long to confront Justine about the fact that Jojo is more than capable of fending for himself when it comes to breakfast. At this point, all my hopes are pinned on the life coach with a fun name. No wonder I'm anxious.

As the doorbell rings sharp and jarring, cutting through the air of the quiet house and demanding attention, I jump in surprise.

Frankie gives my hand a reassuring squeeze as if to say, "this is it". We rise to our feet and head toward the entrance, but little do I know what awaits me on the other side of the door.

When I swung it open to greet Judy, I am taken aback by her appearance. She looks like a cross between Blanche Devereaux from the Golden Girls and Cyndi Lauper. Her green and white polyester jumper is adorned with a gaudy, gold brooch featuring a plethora of colorful rhinestones. Her hair is a wild mop of white, with dark pink tips that stand out in every direction. To top it all off, she is holding a purple hula hoop in one hand and a clipboard, also bedazzled with rhinestones, in the other.

What in the hell have I done?

Frankie nudges me out of my staring stupor. "Hi,

you must be Ms. Shewy," I say, still gawking in wonder at her. I must admit, she definitely seems like she can motivate you to do something other than eat yourself to death. I'm not sure what, but something. Rafa would love this woman with all her vibrant energy.

"And you must be Dessy. Call me Judy."

When she leans in to shake my hand, I can't help but notice the clinking and jingling of the roughly twenty gold bracelets layered on her wrist, creating a sound like that of a human wind chime. I take a step back to allow her to step in, and she takes a good look at Frankie, scanning him from head to toe with an almost discerning gaze.

"You are?" she asks Frankie, handing him her hula hoop. She's smiling like she's the only one that knows a happy secret. I can't help but to like her. I wonder if she has children. Waking up to a mom this bubbly and animated everyday would be exhausting but uplifting, I think.

"Hi, I'm Frankie, Dessy's boyfriend," he says, unsure of what to do with the hula hoop. He moves it back and forth between his hands.

"I'm pleased to meet you both. Could you kindly direct me to the whereabouts of Jojo?" she asks, shifting her body to look around the corner. "I want to get a new mindset going for him as soon as possible. And feel free to use that hula hoop, Frankie. I'm not sure if I'll need it or not. It's kind of an ice breaker when I first meet someone. Watching an old gal like me shimmy that thing up and down her hips can always bust the tension right out of the room."

She sways her hips back and forth dramatically, as if she has an imaginary hula around them, and laughs so hard she lets out a short snort. "I'll let you know," she says as we stand speechless before her.

Frankie speaks up since I'm clearly in shock. "Dessy, can you show Judy to Jojo's room?"

Standing there, I debate on swinging back to last night. Judy seems amazing, but will she understand my brother or even want to. A hula hoop is not going to cut it. Judy would be awesome at running a kids birthday party. I can see that, but I can't see her motivating my brother to do anything.

"Dessy?" Frankie says, and kind of pushes me toward the stairs to snap me out of it.

"Umm, yeah, his room is right up here," I say, giving her no warning that Jojo has no idea she's coming.

I ascend the stairs and lead her behind me. The jangling sound tells me she's following closely. Reaching Jojo's room, I take a step back, almost stepping right on her feet, and open the door for her.

Jojo's facing the wall, seemingly unaware that his door is now open and a complete stranger is staring in at him. He probably thinks I've come to finally lecture him about all the crap he's been eating this week. The room is permeated with the scent of maple syrup, and I notice an empty breakfast plate beside a large bottle of Dr. Pepper.

Judy looks into the abyss of Jojo's room, adjusts her brooch, and clears her throat before making her way inside. I hear her exclaim, "Oh my."

Quickly, I hurry down the stairs and jump into Frankie's lap, snuggling my face into the warm, familiar crook of his neck.

He tenderly wraps his arms around me, offering the comfort and reassurance I desperately need right now. "Well, how do you think this is going to go?" he asks, kissing my forehead with a sigh.

"Terrible," I whisper into his neck, savoring the delightful aroma of vanilla cake that seems to cling to him from the donut shop this morning. It's a calming scent that never fails to lift my spirits. As I cuddle into his embrace, Ponyboy jumps onto the couch, eagerly seeking affection from Frankie. Frankie's the only person Pony doesn't try to take down for some reason, and he has a habit of squeezing himself between us acting as if he's in charge.

Not even a minute later, all hell breaks loose. Jojo's shouts of "get out" and "leave now" are booming from his bedroom like he's yelling into a microphone. Frankie and I leap from the couch and hurry around the corner to investigate the commotion, only to be met by Judy, who clanks down the hallway, gripping her clipboard tightly against her chest. Her forehead is furrowed so deeply that her eyes appear almost closed.

"I apologize, my dear, but it appears I've upset your brother. Perhaps it would be best to leave things be for now," she says apologetically, hurrying toward the door. She pauses briefly to pick up her hula hoop, which is propped against the wall, before shutting the door behind her and taking my hope of better things with her. The fact that we managed to frighten a life coach away tells me we're screwed.

Now what the hell am I going to do?

Chapter Twelve

Before Jojo comes into view, I can hear his labored breathing. He's slowly making his way towards us, gripping the stair rail tightly for support and panting heavily like a freight train trying to climb a hill. The wooden rail is visibly bending under his weight, and I'm afraid it may give way or snap in half, considering how heavily he's leaning on it to support his bum leg.

Frankie moves toward the stairs with the intention of helping Jojo reach us faster, but the sight of Jojo's narrowed eyes, filled with pure rage, stops him in his tracks. To keep his hands occupied, Frankie tightly clenches his fists, unable to bear the sight of someone in need of support and being unable to assist them. I'm certain his anxiety levels are skyrocketing at the sight of Jojo, who is now up and walking despite his injury. Frankie looks from my brother then back to me and finally to the floor. It's not a situation anyone would know how to handle let alone a helper who can do nothing.

"Dessy, I'm going to say this one more time. Butt out of my life," he yells at me and spit flies from his mouth, landing on his chin. "Do you understand me? Butt out!"

I fix my gaze on his unsteady body and cautiously move closer to the bottom of the steps, locking eyes with him. We maintain this intense gaze for a few seconds, and in that moment, his presence on the stairs reminds me of an angry lion, poised to tear me apart limb by limb, but he knows he can't move that fast anymore, and there's a sadness in his eyes that causes me to look down.

"Jo, I need to make something very clear to you. I know, okay? I know that you're completely capable of leaving your room and making your own meals. It's selfish of you to make us wait on you every day, given that you're the one who put yourself in this position," I say firmly, standing up straight again.

With the intention of calming me down, Frankie tries pulling me closer to him by taking my arm.

However, I shake him off and give my brother's angry glare right back to him.

"I put myself in this position? Are you kidding me? Let me tell you something, Dessy. You go around acting like you can fix everything and you have no idea what you're talking about or what I've been through. I never asked you to make my meals or do my laundry! I didn't want any of the food you put in front of me like a prison warden, and I told you that. But you just did what you wanted, not what I wanted."

His whole body is trembling, and he almost loses his balance. His leg will always give him problems, no matter what he weighs, after the type of injury it sustained. "You think criticizing my diet and being the hero for caring so much about my weight makes you the best sister in the world, but it doesn't."

I open my mouth to respond, but I'm stunned by his words.

"Jojo…" Frankie says, but Jojo interrupts him.

"Stay out of it, Frankie."

Frankie nods and backs toward the front door with a downturned mouth and eyes watering from the heartbreak that is taking place right now. Although I'm sure he wants to leave, he'd never abandon me when I'm feeling upset, even if the situation doesn't concern him directly. I think he wishes he could support both me and Jojo right now, but has no idea how.

"Making and forcing healthy meals on me doesn't make you the family champion. It makes you the family bully. You have bullied all of us over something that is none of your concern. This is my life, not yours. When will you get that?"

I start crying now and hard. "How is that bullying? I'm just trying to help. I want you to be okay."

"Then get off your high horse of superiority and let me live my own life. I know I'm a mess. You think I don't see this body?" he says, gesturing to himself. "Do you think that I don't know how to lose weight? I'm an athlete! I know what I look like, and you shoving apples down my throat changes nothing." As he slams his hand down, the rail fractures in two with a sharp crack as the wood fibers separate, and the whole thing falls to the ground with a crash.

"You're not living though. You're killing yourself with food." I'm crying so hard my vision is blurry and my chest aches.

"But who put you in charge of me? You don't get to be the manager of my choices. I want you to leave me alone, and I want that to start now." He turns to go back to his room, and I see two trails of tears streaming down his face. Letting Frankie see him cry is too much for him, and he starts hobbling back to his room, paying no mind to the pile of splintered wood from our banister that he's left all over the stairs.

"Jojo, wait," I say.

He stops, slightly leaning on the wall. He doesn't turn to look at me, but he's no longer moving.

"Can you please just try to see things from my point of view? Can you understand that I love you and I want your life to be better? That's all I was trying to do, Jo, that's all. I never meant to make it worse. I want you to know my intentions were good."

Out of the corner of my eye, I see Frankie nod slowly in agreement. He believes that to be true, because he knows I love my brother dearly.

Jojo slowly turns toward me and says, "Have you for one second put yourself in my shoes? I lost my whole life. If you love me, leave me alone." His chin quivers as he fights to regain his composure.

He's not being fair, and I struggle to come up with an appropriate response as I watch the tears streaming down his plump cheeks speed up and drip onto his shirt. When I don't say anything, he hastily wipes his nose with his sleeve and limps down the hallway, leaving me to contemplate what I could've done differently, knowing I dismissed how he felt about my efforts to help him change his life.

I make my way over to the bottom step where Frankie's cleaning up all the broken wood in sad silence for me and Jojo. I bury my face into my hands, overwhelmed by the gravity of it all.

Frankie's arms envelop me in a warm embrace, but instead of comforting me, it deepens my anguish because I know what I have to do. The only way for Jojo to reclaim his life is for me to go back to the night it was stolen from him. I glance up at Frankie, and he lovingly plants a kiss on each of my cheeks, stopping the tears with his lips before pressing them to mine.

"You tried—you really did. I know you had nothing but the best intentions, and deep down I think Jojo knows that too. He's just tired and overwhelmed by the way things are."

"I tried, but it wasn't enough, and I made him feel worse. I don't know how to help him anymore." My crying starts all over again while I take in deep gulps of air in a complete panic.

The hard part is that I do know how to help him, I just don't like that choice. I don't want to start from the beginning with Frankie. What if I can't?

I wish I knew how to go back and keep Frankie and me just the way we are now, but I don't. If I go back, then I have to live with it all—all the loss I will endure. I'm terrified of going back, but I'm just as terrified to stay. I don't know if Jojo will get better, and I don't want to gamble anymore.

Uncertainty hangs heavy in the air, and I can't bear the thought of continuing to take chances with Jojo's recovery or lack of it. Football was everything to him—it was his passion and his reason for getting up every day—and I possess the power to give it back to him. He's right, I've been selfish, and I can't live with that anymore. I'm confident that if he were in my shoes, he'd do the same for me without hesitation, and that's what I have to do for him.

I pull Frankie's arms tighter around me like a momentary shield from all the brokenness in this house, but I am startled back to reality when I hear the front door open.

It's Justine and oddly enough she is dressed as Cyndi Lauper.

I think to myself Judy Shewy would give her a run for her money in a costume contest. I'd believed Judy Shewy was going to be a game changer for my family, and I couldn't have been more wrong.

I've been a complete idiot.

"What's wrong?" Justine asks, looking from me to Frankie. She pauses in her tracks in confusion at the scene in front of her.

"Jojo and I had an argument."

That is putting it lightly.

She looks down at the broken stair rail, and her jaw drops farther as she stays frozen in shock. She's trying to figure out what exactly is going on, and it seems all she can think to say to me is, "Did you try to give him a snack he hates again?"

A wave of shame washes over me. It's suddenly crystal clear how terrible I've been. Despite thinking I was doing the right thing for months—I've only made things worse for Jojo. Instead of making him feel better, I've been forcing him to confront his pain and sorrow head-on by controlling him in a way that made him feel less than.

Tonight, after everyone has gone to bed, I'm going to travel back to the football game that broke my brother's leg and crushed his spirit. All I can hope is that I can fix Jojo and recreate what I have with the love of my life sitting next to me.

I'm going back for Jojo.

Chapter Thirteen

The warm and humid night has caused my hair to cling to the back of my neck as I sit on the swing, lost in thought for over an hour as I listen to the slight hum of crickets. The crickets are Missouri's way of signaling that summer is coming, and instead of feeling nostalgic, I feel sick. I'm about to swing away my summer with Frankie and go back to the fall of my freshman year before we met.

It's already two o'clock in the morning, and I can't seem to shake off this feeling of dread that has me running through every worst-case scenario possible about swinging back as if I haven't been doing that for the last month. I'm stalling. After making Frankie come over at midnight because I told him I couldn't sleep, I feel worse.

My plan was to just tell him all about going back in time and just suffer whatever those consequences were, but I couldn't do it. I can't risk losing the ability to help Jojo. Frankie must've known I was struggling to tell him something, but I'm sure he assumed it was about what happened with me and my brother earlier. He didn't ask. He just held me in his calm Frankie manner.

How could I ever explain any of this without seeming like a lunatic?

I also had to deal with the strange looks my parents gave me after I confessed to breaking the wooden banister by using it to catch myself when Pony tripped me. They just kept staring at me, then back at the banister, as if trying to make sense of the madness that had taken over the house while they were at work. They didn't even ask me to explain. I'm sure after crying like I had been, they thought I was distraught over it and didn't want to make me feel worse. Frankie assured them he could fix it. My mom simply nodded her head, unsure of what to say, as if she was worried I might do something else that made no sense to anyone. My dad seemed to tiptoe around me for the rest of the night, likely assuming it was just a hormonal breakdown.

It doesn't matter what they think about any of it at this point. I know what I have to do, and that's to swing it all away regardless.

In true Dessy fashion, my heart and brain are divided on this issue. On the one hand, I love Frankie deeply. He was my first love—first everything really—and I was his. Well, not the first kiss, but everything else that followed. I keep telling myself if we have the connection I know in my heart we have, then I can still get that with him again.

I've gone over and over the night we met at Dax Goulart's party. I even went and found the newspaper article my mom kept about my brother being injured and checked what football game we played that night so I can make sure I'm sitting on Dax's back patio, positioning myself in the same place I was two weeks later when Frankie scared me in his Mighty Dogger suit.

Once I go back, I need to find a way to let Jojo know his leg is going to get crushed by number twenty when we play the Ruskin Eagles the night of his injury. It happened in the second half. My plan is to go back to halftime and get to Jojo before that play happens. Creating a distraction to stop the play is what I need to figure out, but I need to tell him why first, without revealing too much. That should be easy enough, I think.

The swing shakes with my trembling. I'm so afraid, and I have nobody to talk to about any of this. This isn't just swinging away a bad day. Swinging away almost four years is like jumping off a cliff and hoping it all works out with your parachute before you hit the bottom. What if going back that far isn't allowed? I'm more afraid that it is allowed. The uncertainty of it all is paralyzing, and I can't help but wonder if there are limitations to this power of mine. What if there are consequences I'm not prepared to face? I feel lost and overwhelmed, wishing there was some sort of manual to guide me through this surreal experience.

I hop off the swing and pace around the yard, trying to make sense of it all… again.

I can do this—I have to do this.

As I stand staring at the sky, I hope for some kind of celestial guidance, a sign that will convince me to abandon this plan. But the stars offer no such message. Frankie's words linger in my mind. He told me that my heart's in the right place when it comes to Jojo, but maybe my help for him needs to look different. He's right, and going back is the only way I can do that at this point. Jojo deserves a second chance.

I clench my teeth, determined to see this through. I stride toward the swing, my thoughts in a whirlwind, and accidentally twist my ankle on a divot in the yard. I lunge for the chains on the swing to catch myself. Good God, I can't even look like a bad ass when I'm changing the world. Luckily, the pain of my ankle will be gone in about thirty seconds.

Hobbling to steady myself, I sink into the swing and close my eyes. As I pump my legs back and forth, adrenaline surges through my whole body. I let my mind go to the worst football game I ever saw. Eyes tightly shut, I focus all my energy on the memory of that halftime. I try imagining the sights and sounds of the football game, the feel of the grass beneath my feet, the tension in the air, and the smell of hot dogs and popcorn coming from the concession stand. I climb higher into the sky and just when I think it's not working, I feel the ground below me quake.

I hop off the swing, staring at my back door, but when I land on my feet, I'm on the sidelines of the football field. The band is marching up and down the field, and the dance team is walking behind me to ready themselves to take over in a gaggle of chatter and laughter. A few seconds pass as I work on getting my bearings with the Friday night lights shining down on me. The buzz of the crowd makes my chest tighten. I glance at the scoreboard, and the score is exactly what it was the night Jojo got hurt. It's all coming back to me.

Jojo's standing next to his coach, leaning in to hear what he's saying. My jaw drops. It's the old Jojo. He's back in his senior year football body. I stare in disbelief. I did it. I actually did it.

A cool shiver runs down my spine, and a prickling sensation spreads all over my back and neck. Instinctively, I gaze downward and extend my arms to inspect myself for a moment. Besides the fact that I'm wearing jeans I don't own anymore, I realize my appearance hasn't undergone too many significant changes. My hair, however, cascades past my shoulders, feeling heavy on my back, catching me off guard since it hasn't been this long since my freshman year.

The starting lineup for the second half is gathering around the coach, eagerly listening to his instructions for the next several plays. They drop down on one knee as the coach retrieves his clipboard and begins outlining his strategies. Every player's eyes are fixed on him with unwavering concentration. The guys are fully absorbed in his game plan and getting hyped up with fist pumps and hollering.

I can sense the steady determination and collective focus on turning this game around because they're currently losing.

My legs quiver uncontrollably beneath me, outwardly showing the fear that has enveloped me. I suppress the panic that threatens to send me home and into a fetal position under every blanket in the house. I am ready to push forward despite the overwhelming sense of dread that has seized me. My stomach churns with nausea, and my thoughts swirl around my mind like marbles tumbling chaotically in a Hungry Hungry Hippos game, released all at once.

Desperately, I pause and draw a few deep breaths, hoping to steady my racing heart and quell the sense of unease that has gripped me. As I regain my composure, I shake off the fear that has paralyzed me and muster the courage to move forward. With each step, I regain my confidence, driven by a fierce determination to overcome the challenge of stopping this game.

It's go time.

CARRIE BEAMER

Chapter Fourteen

"Jojo!" I yell his name, but he doesn't look at me.

"*Jojo!*" I yell again with my hands cupped over my mouth, walking toward him as fast as I can.

He looks up. My eyes lock onto his, but he doesn't meet my gaze, instead choosing to avert his eyes back down. This is any other day to him, but he should at least wonder why I'm down here trying to get his attention.

My heart races with anticipation as I close the distance between us. However, just as I'm about to reach him, the Mighty Dogger runs by me in a blur of fur. Before I can even process what I'm doing, I call out his name. "Frankie!"

The furry wiener dog stops in his tracks, his snarling expression sending a shiver down my spine and not in a bad way. That's my Frankie in there. I want to run to him, jump in his fluffy arms, and bury away what I've done. But I'm frozen in fear. I didn't know Frankie until a couple of weeks after Jojo got hurt. Memories of Jojo's injury come flooding back to me, the weight of guilt and regret laying on my chest like a heavy boulder.

As the seconds tick by with Frankie staring at me through his mask, the heat of embarrassment creeps up my face, and I become painfully aware of the dance team shimmying past us, their rhythmic movements providing a sharp contrast to my own frozen state.

A muffled "oh hey" comes from the dog head, and he sort of waves one paw, trying to place who I am— we don't have any classes together.

"Hey," I say and turn on my heels toward Jojo with my heart in my throat, hoping Frankie moves on. Anxiety washes over me in waves as I contemplate the gravity of what I've just done. My mind races with questions and doubts, wondering if I have just altered the course of the universe by meeting him before I was meant to. Despite the chaos raging inside me, I know that I must move forward and get to my brother.

By the time I get to the huddle, Jojo's no longer standing there. I interrupt the coach, looking around frantically. How did I lose him already? "Where's my brother?"

He stares at me in annoyance, and I realize he probably has no clue who my brother is or cares.

"I'm looking for Jojo Ortega?"

He waves me off and says, "He's in the can."

The can? I turn in a circle before I hear Trey Gibson say, "He went to the potty." The group of guys all laugh, slapping each other in celebration of their stupidity.

Why are boys so exasperating?

"Thanks," I say as I start running, not caring what anyone thinks. I have to warn Jojo even though he won't have any way of knowing why or how I know what's going to happen. I can't worry about that part of it. I just have to tell him things are about to go very wrong and hope to hell he trusts me.

Behind me, I hear the whistle blow. I turn back to see Jojo sprinting toward me, strapping his helmet on.

Catching my breath, I stop and try to block his path. It's still jarring to see him so healthy and back in a football uniform. "Hey, Jo, I need to tell you something, and I need you to listen to me." I put my arms out in front of me to stop him as he gets closer.

He flies right past me and hollers, "Not now, Des. They need me on the field."

I stand in disbelief. Shit, shit, shit! I'll never catch him. I need a new plan, and I need it now.

I think back to precisely when number twenty came at my brother with his disgusting dirty tackle. Jojo was making a break for the end zone, and it was very close to the beginning of the second half, like minutes maybe even seconds. I speed walk—so I don't draw any more attention to myself—to the sideline closest to the end zone and wait, still out of breath. My freshman body was not in great shape when it came to cardio apparently.

To prevent this impending nightmare from becoming a reality, I realize that resorting to doing something completely ludicrous is my only option. Fortunately, no one has attempted to push me back toward the stands, so I can focus on the task at hand without any issues. I don't have time for any obstacles. I need to become the obstacle.

I clench my fists and ready myself for the play. Briefly, I glance up to see if I can spot my dad in the stands. I know he's there somewhere with his school spirit sweatshirt and hat on. He's never missed any of my brother's games. Unlike the last time, it won't be my dad rushing onto the field. This time, it's up to me to take charge. If my dad happens to make his way down here, it'll be because he thinks his daughter has gone completely insane, and in all honesty, he wouldn't be wrong.

In the midst of turning my gaze back toward the field, the moment I have been dreading materializes before my eyes. Jojo expertly receives Dax's exceptional throw, and he's swiftly on his way to the end zone. Without a second thought, I bolt across the field, my hair thrashing wildly behind me. I've never run so fast in my entire life. My arms flail uncontrollably as I repeatedly bellow for them to stop at the top of my lungs. It's like an out of body experience. I've never even walked onto this football field before, let alone flown across it during a live game.

As I turn and charge toward the end zone to catch up with my brother and number twenty, players abruptly halt on the field as I come into their sight line, startled by my frenzied sprint in front of them. Suddenly, I stumble over my own feet, hurtling headfirst to the ground and executing a full-blown somersault before arriving in the end zone. Despite the rough landing, I manage to sit up just in time for the referee to blow his whistle. I'm certain he's contemplating how to address the situation of a deranged girl infiltrating the field, but his perplexed face is looking to the players for some sort of help in understanding what course of action he needs to take next. This is a first for all of us I'm guessing. My neck feels out of whack, and my elbow has skin missing where I burned it across the turf.

"Have you lost your mind?" Jojo asks when he gets to me. He's out of breath and still cradling the football. He looks like he's not sure if it's actually his sister sitting on the football field. He is looking at me and then back at everyone else in disbelief.

I can't answer because Frankie—in his Mighty Dogger suit—is coming toward me with one paw reaching out to me. I'm not sure what to do so, I take his paw and let him pull me to standing while I catalogue what else I hurt in my run for the end zone.

"What the hell, Dessy! You just ruined the best touchdown of my life." Jojo's nostrils are flared, and his eyes are narrowed. I know this look of rage on his face all too well. It's the same look he gave me when Frankie cut a hole in our wall.

I don't speak. I'm too busy staring at Frankie or I should say the Mighty Dogger. I strain to catch a glimpse of his eyes through the mesh of his dog head, hoping to gauge his reaction to me. I'm expecting comfort from him that he doesn't know I need. He remains silent behind his mask of fur.

As I take a step back, knowing this moment needs to be quashed, I express my gratitude with a quick thank you before turning my focus back to my brother, who now stands alongside his irate teammates, glaring daggers at me.

"I ... I thought there was a dog on the field, and I didn't want anyone to get hurt." I shrug my shoulders, disappointed I couldn't come up with something better. I'm not sure it would matter what I said at this point. A ruined play is a ruined play.

"A dog? Are you kidding me? That's the only dog on the field," says number twenty from the Eagles, laughing as he points at the back of Frankie walking away in his Mighty Dogger suit.

I lower my eyes at this creep. This jackass is literally the whole entire reason I'm back in my freshman year, enduring this torturous experience all over again. I ball my hands into fists and force myself to walk away in silence. I don't have anything else to say, and I want to get the hell out of here. The stands of people above me are noisy with chatter as everyone wants to understand what just happened. I try not to look anywhere but in front of me.

Even though I successfully put an end to the play, I can't shake the feeling of helplessness that's taken hold of me. The gravity of my situation sinks in. I'm faced with the daunting reality of reliving almost four years of my life all over again. The overwhelming dread that consumes me is almost unbearable. I could cry and throw up both at the same time.

Glancing toward the sideline, I see my dad standing expectantly right where I'd anticipated he'd be with his hat being passed back and forth between his hands nervously, but my attention is quickly drawn back to Frankie. He's removed his mascot head and appears to be in deep conversation with one of the cheerleaders. As I get closer to them, their conversation becomes more discernible, and I overhear the cheerleader expressing her admiration to Frankie for his gallant rescue of helping me up on the field.

A sickening awareness dawns on me— she's flirting with him. The thought alone is enough to send my mind reeling, and I feel a pit forming in my stomach. No, no, no, this can't be happening. My worst fear is confirmed when I notice the unmistakable signs of interest on Frankie's face.

He's grinning, showing off his dimples and leaning in closer to hear her better.

I can hardly believe what I'm witnessing. This can't be happening. Isn't the universe supposed to reward me with good things for helping my brother? Instead, I'm seeing a nightmare unfold in front of me.

He turns his head and watches me walk past him, causing my mind to go blank. I'm left with a dilemma— should I abandon the initial plan of meeting him at Dax's party in a few weeks and approach him now? The thought of scrapping the original plan and taking matters into my own hands is tempting, because I'm not sure if it would cause a different outcome given that we've already met. Waiting for the party may cost me the chance to get him back as there's now an adorable cheerleader in the mix, and I can tell there's a spark between them. It feels like a knife straight to my heart. Plus, I don't know how long this has gone on between them. Days? Weeks?

It doesn't help that my dad's yelling my name and waving his arms insanely, ushering me over to him. I'm sure he's dying to know why I decided to stop my brother's football game. I'm going to tell him I saw a dog—that's my story and I'm sticking to it.

"Hey, that somersault you pulled off in the end zone should be watched and admired by every NFL player in the world. Seriously impressive."

When Frankie says this to me, I know he's being for real. He isn't making fun of me—he'd never make fun of anyone. He's probably trying to make me—a girl he doesn't know yet—feel better about what just happened.

I give him a slow, wide grin, the one I know he likes. "Thanks, but I'm pretty sure the whole team wants to kill me."

"Nah. They're just bummed you didn't have the ball in your hands when you did it. But honestly you should maybe have your head checked for a concussion. You looked like you might have banged it kind of hard." I melt when I see a look of concern spread across his face, knowing that concern is for me and my possible concussion once again. Frankie is the same person no matter what year it is. I love him so much. For the second time tonight, I want to run to him and shower him with kisses. Going to him would make me look even crazier than running on the field just did. I know that, but I'm struggling with letting it go.

My dad, being my dad, is more concerned with the beating my body took falling on the field then why I did it. He has to be the most loving dad out there—sometimes to a fault. Maybe if he would've stayed on top of Jojo after his injury none of this would've happened. I shake away the thought. It's not healthy to go around holding grudges and casting blame on others for things that have already transpired.

I remind myself that I made a conscious decision to return to this night, and it's now my responsibility to move forward. Despite this logical reasoning, I struggle to convince my heart to let go of the anger and frustration that still linger within me like ghosts of the past. And being in love with Frankie while watching him with someone else is going to undo me. That's not something I saw coming, and I know I can't handle it.

Despite the pang of longing and heartache I feel from my run in with Frankie, I know that I have to push those emotions aside and focus on the mission to get him back. I helped Jojo so now figuring out Frankie is my only focus.

With my dad by my side, I make my way to the stands, hoping to distract myself from the prying stares of those around me. It's difficult to ignore the attention I'm getting over storming the field just minutes ago. Instead, I immerse myself in the game, cheering alongside the other spectators and reveling in the excitement of the moment. Thank God we're winning now, because me stopping the play right before my brother scored would've made me a major target of school spirit gone wrong.

After enduring an hour of stares and gossip from the people around me, Dad and I shuffle off the bleachers with the rest of the happy crowd. My stunt tonight will hopefully be left in the past since we ended up killing the Eagles in the second half thirty-four to seven.

I get another jolt of surprise when I see Justine standing in the parking lot with some friends, looking radiant and carefree with her long hair curled and makeup on. It's a stark contrast to the solemn and reserved person I've grown accustomed to seeing after my brother's injury. It's only now that I realize just how much she has changed in the intervening years. My heart swells with a bittersweet mix of emotions as I watch her tilt her head back and burst into a joyous fit of laughter. It's a sound I've not heard in what feels like an eternity, and the warmth it brings to my heart is quickly tempered by the knowledge of all that we've lost in the process. This was the right decision. I know it now. I just need to find a way to get my boyfriend back before he falls in love with someone else.

Then all at once, I remember.

I have Rafa back!

CARRIE BEAMER

Chapter Fifteen

I stop running when I reach Rafa's front yard and take it all in. I haven't been here since he moved to California. To be honest, I avoided it as much as I could because it made me long for him.

I look up toward the towering, sunflower-colored house that looms above me. The white shutters that adorn its windows are peeling, and it's clear that many of the blinds are missing slats. One window in particular catches my eye, where a red blanket has been hastily hung in place of the absent blinds. I don't remember that hanging in the window before.

As I take in the dilapidated state of the house, that seems pretty much the same as it did the last time I was here, I notice that the front screen door is swaying in the wind, hanging crookedly from its hinges just like ours is—Missouri wind loves to ruin screen doors. The passage of time is evident in the weathered appearance of the several lawn chairs scattered haphazardly across the expansive front porch. Despite the faded, worn-out quality of the chairs, they seem almost timeless, as though they've been a fixture of the porch for many years.

I let myself in, trying to hop around the white powder deodorizer his foster mom Barb sprinkles on the carpet. Sometimes, she lets it sit for two days before vacuuming it up. It makes the whole house smell like a potpourri bomb mixed with wet dog. I don't know how Rafa breathes in here.

With my powder-covered socks, I scurry down to the room Rafa shares with a kid named Billy that's never here. I find him sprawled out on his bed, a notebook resting on his lap as he jots down notes, his headphones plugged into the stereo.

My mom put the stereo on layaway last year and bought it for him for Christmas. Jojo and I didn't even care that our Christmas was less because of that stereo. Rafa deserves it. It's his most prized possession.

I take a running leap from the doorway. I fling myself on his back and wrap my arms around his whole body like a giant bear would hug its children.

"What in the Chaka Khan is going on?" he says, trying to look back at me while I straddle his back.

I try playing it off that I'm acting like I haven't seen him in years. "Nothing's going on." I try imagining what facial expression I have plastered across my face right now as I roll off his back and sit up.

"You look like you just won a million bucks but found out it was stolen. You're kind of weirding me out. Why are you gawking at me like that?"

He laughs and carefully removes his headphones, treating them with a tenderness reserved for delicate China. It's clear that these headphones are his escape from reality. It's no surprise that he spends most of his time in his room with them on, lost in melodies that transport him to another world far away from the current no family state he lives in. When he's not working at the record store, he can always be found in this very spot, the headphones firmly in place, as he immerses himself in the artistry of music.

It didn't break his heart to move to California. With aspirations of soaring to great heights as a musician once he graduates from high school, there's little doubt in my mind he'll make his dreams a reality. His unbelievable talent for music is awe-inspiring, and he can seamlessly play almost any instrument handed to him. His vocal ability, however, is otherworldly. As soon as he sings, his voice is nothing short of mesmerizing, stopping anyone who happens to be in earshot dead in their tracks. It's a voice that is at once smooth and powerful, yet somehow impossibly light.

Our choir teacher, Mr. James, is ready for Rafa to be on Broadway. He told him before he moved to California not to ever rule out Broadway. Mr. James felt the weight of Rafa leaving almost as heavily as I did. Rafa had been the shining star of every school musical, his talent and passion for music infectiously spreading to every student who had the opportunity to perform alongside him.

"I just missed you. Can't I miss my best friend?"

"I mean you can, but you just saw me a couple of hours ago, but I get it, I'm fly," he says, dusting his deep purple polished nails on his jeans like royalty.

I throw a pillow at him that he dodges effortlessly.

Finding a way to get Rafa up to speed without telling him I'm here from the future is gonna be tricky. Just thinking about that makes me laugh and shudder at once.

"Now what are you laughing about? Have you been dabbling in herbal things I should know about? Cuz you're on another level tonight." He looks at me and tilts his head sideways, trying to figure me out. I suppose I am acting like a lunatic in his eyes.

"So, I sort of talked to a guy tonight that I think is…"

I'm trying to think of how to describe Frankie in a way that doesn't sound like I already know him. I'm also avoiding telling Rafa that I ran like a freak onto the football field. He already thinks I'm being strange tonight. How would I explain that act of insanity? He'll hear about it soon enough at school Monday, which will really leave me a mess to explain.

I know kids aren't forgetting about that anytime

soon.

"What? Really? Who is it?"

Rafa pauses his music and gives me his full attention as soon as I bring up the topic of a guy. He's intrigued, but I can't help but feel a bit self-conscious. After all, Rafa's the one who tends to jump from relationship to relationship, not me. I had a few boyfriends back in middle school, but I quickly discovered they were all a bunch of sweaty, smelly liars. Rafa likes to remind me that most kids our age are liars, but he still enjoys making out with them anyway. I couldn't decide if that was true after having my eighth grade heart broken by Lorenzo Whipple. That boy played games, and I was done with all of them after him—until I met Frankie. I hate that in this moment there's so much I know that Rafa doesn't.

"It's not a big deal. It's our mascot, you know the Mighty Dogger?"

Rafa gazes up at the ceiling, lost in thought for a moment, before a smile spreads across his face. He nods approvingly and even claps his hands, clearly happy to hear that I'm out of my "guy slump".

"Oh yeah, that's Frankie Rubio. He's in my English class. Nice guy." He smiles wider. "And he's cute as hell. He must've gone to a different middle school than us. I don't remember him."

I want to gush about Frankie and have to physically bite my lip. "I kind of tripped onto the field tonight and he helped me up." I might as well just come out with it.

"You fell on the field?" he asks, smacking his forehead with the palm of his hand. "I don't even want to know," he says, waving the thought away with his hands like he's batting away a bunch of tiny gnats in his face.

"So, do you think he's interested in you? Did you

have a chance to talk to him? Or was it just a brief interaction?" Rafa asks, clearly curious to know whether Frankie is interested in me or not. He leans into me intently.

Trying to think of how to answer his questions about the love of my life who, at this point in time, doesn't even know my name, is making me sweat a little.

"I don't know if he's interested in me, but I want him to be." I smile my slyest smile, and he slaps his bed in excitement.

"That's what I'm talking about, Des! If you like him, then I say you need to go after him and fast. I'm surprised he hasn't been snatched up by now."

The comfort and security that comes with Rafa's unconditional support never fails to amaze me. He doesn't need a reason to stand by me. He just believes in me and that's enough. It hurts to know that our time together is limited, but I take solace in the fact that our friendship will stand the test of time and distance. Rafa and I share a bond that goes beyond the physical realm. It's like our souls are intertwined. I've never been as close to anyone as I have with Rafa, until Frankie came along. He adored Frankie when we got together because of who Frankie is, so I know he will adore him again.

"Okay, so what exactly does "going after him" look like? I'm not in the practice of going after anyone." I ask, because Frankie and I getting together wasn't forced. It just happened, and I wish it could happen like that again. I'm pretty sure I already messed that up, though.

"Let me see, where would he hang out?" He taps his fingernails on his chin in thought. "Oh, I know! He goes to Pete's after Friday night games with the football team. I saw him last weekend when I went back inside to grab some extra pickles Jake conveniently forgot to give you, probably in the hopes of seeing you again. There he was, just hanging around like a gigolo holding your cup of pickles. But I definitely remember seeing Frankie in line."

"I don't remember seeing him," I say, because I was in the future last Friday for God's sake. This is ridiculous, and I can tell it is going to get quite confusing.

"I do, because he had the Mighty Weiner head or Mighty Dogger, or whatever, sitting on the top of someone's car when I came back out. Remember? Sheesh, talk about someone who lives the part. I admire that actually. Go all in or don't go at all," he says, nodding with pride. Rafa loves anyone who gives it all they have.

His face drops.

"What? Why are you frowning?" My heart flutters with panic.

"I think he was there with a cheerleader. I remember seeing him with one in line."

"Well, maybe they're just friends."

A dark cloud of dread slowly envelops me, suffocating me with its weight. I wrack my brain, trying to recall any mention of a cheerleader, specifically the one I saw him talking to tonight, in Frankie's past but draw a blank. What if my presence here has drastically changed the course of events, leading Frankie to fall in love with someone else, someone he was never meant to be with? I can't bring myself to be that girl, the one who meddles and tries to break up a couple. It's just not who I am. But he's my Frankie, dammit.

"You're probably right." He nods but isn't convincing me at all with that frown getting bigger.

"Hey, I have an idea." I get some excitement back.

"Go on." As he leans back against his headboard, crossing his legs at the ankles, he pauses for a moment, listening keenly for the sound of his foster mom's footsteps on the stairs. She is a kind woman who always goes out of her way to bring us snacks. She tries to give Rafa a normal life as best she can.

My stomach growls at the thought of the butter crackers smothered with canned squirt cheese that his foster mom always brings up. I love the taste of the cheese, but Rafa gags when I eat it. He can't understand how anyone can like fake cheese from a can. The only thing missing from the cracker cheese snack is a pickle on top. The combination of the tangy pickle and the creamy cheese would be one hell of a snack. I don't know how I forgot all about that squirty cheese. I need to go in search of this once we make a plan.

"So, like I told you, he helped me up tonight. Maybe I can write him a note thanking him, and you can give it to him in English on Monday?"

"*Lame*," Rafa says, dragging the word out way longer than necessary.

"Why is that lame? Plus, if he does have a girlfriend, there's no harm in thanking him."

"Oh, there's harm in it with the way you look so dreamy right now." He chuckles and thinks for a second. "I guess his response to the note would tell us if he's interested in you," he says, conceding.

He better be interested in me, I think. How could he not be interested in me? This is all too much.

Rafa leans down, his hand reaching for one of the many notebooks strewn about his room, each containing music lyrics he's been working on. He picks one up and tosses it to me along with a pen, urging me to get started. "Don't keep me waiting," he says with a grin. "I need to see if I approve of this letter before I go making a spectacle of myself handing a note to a boy who might just end up being your prom date someday."

Holding the notebook and pen, my mind drifts to the memory of my first prom with Frankie. The mere mention of prom sends a wave of emotions through me that is hard to contain. I want to pour my heart out to Rafa and tell him every detail of that magical night. My mind instantly goes to how Frankie surprised me by picking me up in a limousine and taking me to a park we both loved instead of to a fancy restaurant. The interior of the limo was beautifully decorated with flowers, and he'd even packed a picnic basket with all my favorite dishes his mom makes. But the two slices of his grandmother's cinnamon caramel cake that is to die for was the best part of the meal.

My mom made me the most stunning deep purple satin gown with a fitted bodice, but the bottom had a gentle A-line shape that flared out from my waist and fell so gracefully to the floor. I felt beautiful and Frankie eyes gleamed when he saw me. I will never forget how he seemed to hold his breath when I came down the stairs into the entry of my house. My hair was pinned up, and Justine had painted my nails a lavender shade called Lavender Sky to offset the darkness of my dress.

We sat in the limo at the park and ate and talked for two hours before the dance. He understood what I wanted my prom experience to be, and it wasn't piling into the Olive Garden with the rest of our friends. I craved the intimate night he gave me.

That magical prom night I realized how much Frankie meant to me. From that moment on, I knew that my life wouldn't be complete without him. He has this effortless way of making me feel happy and at ease, even in the most mundane situations. I long to be with him right now, to feel his reassuring presence and see his smiling face. I want to take in his wonderful, sweet coffee vanilla scent.

Rafa clears his throat, interrupting my thoughts as I realize I've been holding the pen and notebook with glazed over eyes for probably five minutes.

"Wow, you do have it bad for him. Put your creative writing skills to use and write him a note that's perfect. Tell him thank you and throw in some Dessy flair. You want to be a writer, so let's see what ya got." He snaps his fingers in the air to get me going.

I nod and smile. I know just what to say, because I'm not writing a note to a boy I just met.

I'm writing to my Frankie.

CARRIE BEAMER

Chapter Sixteen

As I pace back and forth across my room, I keep one eye fixated on Pony, who is situated nearby just watching me curiously. I can't get my body to unwind and relax for the night. It seems as though Pony's aware of this too. He keeps sniffing in my direction, sensing that something is amiss. I can't help but notice how much Pony has changed since I came back. He looks so much younger and skinnier than I remember him being, and this realization only adds to my growing unease.

"You're welcome, I gave you your youth back," I say to him, hands on my hips as I loom over him.

He meows as if to say, "Lady, I know what you did."

He knows.

From my window, I can see Jojo and Justine on the driveway. They're locked in an intense make-out session, their heated antics steaming up the windows of Jojo's truck. I glare down at them, grossed out, as if they'd even notice my disapproving looks.

Her pink lace bra is draped across his dashboard, and it's surprising to see how fast they've moved, considering they haven't been dating for very long. Well, not at this point, but I guess it's comforting to know it works out. How are they not worried my parents will peek out and see them too? No one wants their parents seeing them in the throes of teen passion. I guess Frankie and I played it safe, and clearly Jojo doesn't care. I'm so happy Jojo is back to his old, outgoing self, but I'm angry that they have each other, and I have nothing. I sink onto my bed after tripping over Ponyboy—some things didn't change.

It's Friday night and wondering where Frankie is

at this very moment is tearing me up. Is he with the cheerleader? Has he kissed her? Is it serious? Rafa's probably asleep by now, because I made him continuously read the note I kept rewriting Frankie over and over. I want it to be perfect, and I think I exhausted him with the whole thing. I debate walking over to talk to him, but I've been crying, and he'll know immediately. I can't tell him I'm upset over Frankie. Crying over a guy I supposedly just met would make me look extremely desperate.

I try laying down under my blankets and taking deep breaths, but I find myself experiencing intense waves of anxiety that shake through me like seismic tremors. It's as if my entire being is caught in the grip of a massive earthquake of fear and apprehension, and I can't seem to find any relief. My body and brain don't feel right—I'm not myself. It's like my thoughts grew and matured as I went through high school, but now I've taken it backward. I sit up and shake out my arms as if that's going to help anything. I try some deep breathing exercises, and I finally fall asleep.

****

As the weekend slowly drags on, I find myself holed up at my parent's shop, desperately trying to distract myself from the impending reality check that awaits me at school tomorrow when Rafa gives Frankie the note I wrote him.

It's almost Halloween and we're swamped, but it does help keep my mind busy a bit, though not enough. This note could be the dumbest idea yet. Thinking about all the strange turn of events that brought me back to this time, I can't help but wonder if there's some greater purpose at play. Perhaps everything happens for a reason, and I need to trust in the process even when it seems impossibly difficult. This is easier said than done.

The note I wrote Frankie basically says I appreciate the fact that he helped a girl up who seemed to have momentarily lost her mind and that I'm sorry I didn't thank him properly on Friday. I ended the note by saying I would be at Pete's on Monday night and would love to thank him with a burger. I didn't add with extra pickles, but I wanted to.

My note isn't flirty. That's not the way to get his attention. He's not one for shallow crap like flirty notes from someone he doesn't even know. Rafa basically told me my note seems forward as hell, asking him to meet for a burger. He said I need to learn to play hard to get, but this is Frankie, my Frankie. I know him. He won't think I'm being forward—he'll assume I'm genuine. He'll like that I took the time to say thank you and invite him to Pete's. He's just a good person who doesn't think people play games. Knowing him like I do is the only thing I have going for me.

I also know him well enough to know he'll feel obligated to go to Pete's. His kind heart would never let him blow anyone off or hurt their feelings. Rafa applauded my confidence, but I could sense he was harboring doubts about the outcome of my bold invitation to Frankie. The possibility of rejection looms large in my mind, threatening to crush my self-esteem and leave me feeling utterly devastated. What if this Frankie isn't exactly my Frankie?

Despite Rafa's words of encouragement, I find myself constantly oscillating between two conflicting scenarios. On the one hand, I can't shake the feeling that maybe Frankie will show up and we'll reconnect on a deep and meaningful level, just like we used to. On the other hand, the nagging doubt in my mind keeps whispering that Frankie will only want to be friends, leaving me in a painful state of limbo with no hope for a deeper connection.

As I contemplated the possible outcomes, I know deep down that I could never settle for just friendship if I know there is no chance for a deeper relationship. The thought of being stuck in a one-sided relationship that can never evolve into something more is simply too painful to bear.

Even with all my fears and doubts, I know I have to be true to myself and take a chance on love. Whatever the outcome, I am determined to stay strong and hold onto the hope that the future held the promise of something better. The promise of me and Frankie.

By the time I get home, I'm just ready to pass out in bed. I try not to think about school and whether or not Frankie will indeed meet me at Pete's after Rafa gives him the note. Glancing at my nightstand where I've had a picture of Frankie and I for three years, I see nothing but some new black, sparkly Avon nail polish my mom ordered for Rafa from the Halloween Avon catalog the neighbor down the street leaves on our door once a month. I sigh loudly and Ponyboy sighs with me. That picture isn't there because the day it was taken hasn't happened yet.

I can see that picture in my mind so clearly. Frankie had talked me into volunteering at school cleanup day—of course he did. You arrive on a Saturday at the designated location assigned to you, geared up and ready to tackle tasks like trimming overgrown shrubs, painting walls, or cleaning out the cluttered library shelves. Even though it was a day filled with manual labor and hard work, which left me totally exhausted and drenched in sweat, it was one of the best days spent with Frankie. I didn't have bad days with him. It was always good with us.

There were so many little moments with him on

school cleanup day as we grew to know each other that I remember. We were taking a water break and chatting when a girl from the yearbook committee snapped a picture of us, sweaty and leaning on the back of the school wall. Frankie was laughing with his head tipped sideways, looking at me, and I was beaming. That picture captured 'Frankie and I for who we are together, always cracking up and completely happy even covered in dirt and sweat. Is that picture floating out in the atmosphere someplace waiting to be summoned back to me in three years? Will we still do school cleanup day together a couple of months from now?

Two days ago, he kissed me outside my house before I swung back to now. I replay the kiss in my mind, running my fingertips over my mouth. I can almost feel his lips on mine. Tears pour down my face hot and salty, seeping into my neck. I tremble and wonder if I can swing forward to a time that has already happened. I want to go back. I can't do this for Jojo. I want my life back. Ponyboy crawls onto my chest and nuzzles his face in my hand to calm me down. I guess he's good for something sometimes even if he'd trip me if I got up to get a tissue.

I let myself cry it out and somehow that helps me finally calm myself down and focus on the plan I've put in place. Rafa will give Frankie the note, and I'll go to Pete's tomorrow night and hope to hell he shows up so I can make him see in me what he did when we fell in love. I need to take this one day at a time or I'll lose my sanity, but first I need to get some ice to reduce my swollen eyes. I can't show up to school looking like Rocky Balboa after nine rounds.

CARRIE BEAMER

Chapter Seventeen

The start of school is bizarre—I imagine this'll be a running theme since I came back to freshman year. Sitting in the same classes I took three years ago will be like falling into a well I can't get out of. I know I'm not supposed to be here, but I can't do anything about it but wait and improve my grades, I guess.

The weirdest part is that my schedule is in a completely different order then when I was a freshman before. I have the same classes, but the hours are different. I found this out the hard way when I sat down in Mrs. Suttner's class second period, and everyone was staring at me. Then Mrs. Suttner kindly let me know I had her class sixth hour and asked me if I need a pass to the health room. I left with looks of concern written all over everyone's faces, including mine.

I am currently standing in the counseling office while the secretary Ms. Rodebush writes my schedule down for me.

I can see the worry in her eyes as she takes out her notebook and glances up at me with every line she writes. We'd already been in school for almost three months when I came back to the football game to save Jojo, and I should know my schedule by now. She hands it to me and says, "Everything okay, hon?"

I nod and get the hell out of there. I am clearly not okay, but there's nothing she can do about it. I can't imagine what my school counselor would say if I told her I'm a time traveler. School counselors deal with enough struggling kids, they don't need my drama.

I watch as Cathy Boyle is bullied by the same two boys who have mercilessly taunted her about her acne condition since the seventh grade. They call her pizza face and pretend to pop zits on her skin. I hate it for her and tell them to shut up. I smile and tell Cathy, "Just wait until senior year. You're going to knock them dead."

She looks at me and says, "Thank you?" She looks confused but appreciates the support.

Little does she know that her senior year will usher in a remarkable turn of events that will see her crowned as the prom queen. She will become the most adored and popular girl in our entire school. Her exceptional compassion, coupled with her unrelenting commitment to selflessly going above and beyond for others, will unquestionably capture the hearts of everyone around her. This makes me think of Frankie. He's a total Cathy Boyle.

****

"Girl, what in the name of single chicks everywhere are you going for here?" Rafa looks me up and down when I get to his house.

I'd gone home after school and attempted to make myself over into something I'm not. I always over makeup when I'm nervous, especially now that I have to work around some acne again. The difference now is that I'm back to freshman year. That means I have the same stupid makeup Rafa got rid of and replaced for me my sophomore year. I'm a total mess. "What do you mean? I say, looking down at myself and patting my hair even though I know he's right.

"You're done up like you're being featured in a Debbie Gibson music video. Why the hell did you blow your sides out like that? You trying to catch some wind and fly your butt to Pete's with that hair? And your makeup is screaming "help, I need a boyfriend". I need to fix this now. You need to drab down. Less is more unless you're on a stage, which you are not. When will people get that?"

He runs a comb through all the hairspray I used to blow out my sides while handing me a tissue to wipe away some of the makeup, mumbling the whole time in annoyance with my efforts. "We're getting you a new lip color tomorrow after school. This pink is not working for you. I don't think this pink works for anyone. It's just ick."

I smile, remembering the day he replaced my makeup before, but under very different circumstances. "I just want to make sure he notices me," I say, desperate for him to understand how much I love Frankie without seeming like a clinger.

"Oh, he'll notice you alright, like a rabid dog notices a squirrel in the yard. That's not what you're going for."

I wish someone on this planet knew what was happening to my life. Can I tell Rafa? Should I at least try explaining myself? I need to think about this more. Right now, I have twenty minutes to get to Pete's to see if Frankie shows up.

Rafa said Frankie read the note and said, "Cool, thanks." He gave Rafa a nod and slipped it into his pocket. Just hearing him tell me Frankie read it gave me butterflies in my chest while my stomach dropped with dread and excitement. My body doesn't know how to react to any of my jumbled thoughts and feelings.

By the time we get to Pete's, I've worked myself into a full-on fit of panic. We even had to stop on the way so Rafa could rub my temples with his thumbs and tell me to breathe. He's not used to seeing me this way, and his wrinkled brow tells me he's not sure what the hell is going on. He appears worried I'm going through something else. And he's right—I am. But Rafa has no family and lives in a foster home, and here I am acting like a guy is the biggest problem in the world. I'm an idiot even if he'd never make me feel that way.

I hear Frankie before I see him. It's his laugh I recognize coming from the front door. He's in black stone-washed jeans and a Culture Club sweatshirt. He looks amazing but different somehow. It's not that he looks years younger than I'm used to, because obviously he does. His shoulders and whole stance are altered, and it's strange.

I shake it off and my heart sinks when I see he's with the same cheerleader he was talking to Friday night. This was my biggest fear leading up to tonight.

"Okay, don't look desperate to talk to him. Just act like I'm telling you a story and be cool," Rafa says as we stand near the front with some other kids playing Pac-Man and surveying music on the jukebox.

"How will I offer to buy him a burger if I don't go say hi?"

"Just hold your water. It's not time for all of that yet. I want to see if he notices you first. I'm trying to figure out if he's dating this cheerleader. I think her name is Audrey," he says, squinting his eyes at them but then turning away quickly.

I quickly glance back at them before Frankie looks at me. "He's not dating her," I say.

"How do you know?" Rafa's completely staring at them now.

"Oh my God stop looking. I know because they aren't holding hands." I grin to myself. Frankie held my hand anytime we were out and about. He even held my hand riding in his jeep.

"Hello there, oh radiant being of hotness," Jake utters with a hint of sass in his voice as he executes a smooth moonwalk in his white Converse back to the counter. He seems to believe that he is the epitome of cool. "So, when are you going to let me take you out for a movie?" he asks with a mischievous smile, raising a single eyebrow in a suggestive manner as he gazes at me.

"Ugh, can you just not today?" Rafa says and puts his hand up in Jake's face. "You're being a try hard and it's off-putting, Jake. Lord, you need to get some respect for yourself. *She is not interested.*"

Jake has no comeback to that. Rafa has once again put him in his place.

"Hi, Dessy," I hear Frankie say from behind me, and I want to cry and hug him.

Rafa murmurs, "Girl, it's time."

What would I do without Rafa? Actually, I already know the answer to that.

"Hey, it's you," I say, turning to face Frankie and Audrey or Aubrey. I'm not sure which it is.

I'm a freak. Why would I say "hey it's you"? *Pull yourself together, Dessy.*

"Uh, yeah." He smiles, and I get lost in the depths of his blue eyes.

"I don't know about you guys, but I'm here for my onion ring fix," Rafa says, trying to normalize my odd behavior. He subtly elbows me in the side.

A sudden sense of assertiveness surges within me, and I stride confidently toward the counter.

"What can I get your hotness today," Jake says, and I honestly want to punch him in the throat.

Rafa's stern attitude only kept Jake down for so long. The guy is exceedingly bothersome.

I turn to Frankie. "Frankie, I'm totally buying you a burger," I say and then look back at Audrey. "And you too Audrey ... Aubrey? What do you guys want?"

"It's Aubrey," she says, crossing her arms over her chest in a mildly annoyed manner. I get a closer look at her and she's cute. Dammit, I was hoping she wasn't as cute as I thought she was when I saw her on the football field. She has that blonde hair with adorable freckles sprayed across her nose look. I am literally her complete opposite.

Although I'm fully aware of Frankie's burger order, it would be awkward for me to order his food for him, which comprises of a double cheeseburger with ketchup and extra pickles. I go ahead and order my own burger, patiently waiting for him to place his own like we haven't stood together in this line a million times before.

Frankie pulls out his wallet. "You don't have to do that, Dessy."

Aubrey's wearing a slight scowl, looking confused and probably wondering why she's standing in line being offered food from a girl she only knows in passing at school. I ignore her questioning looks and turn my attention to Frankie. I'm not here to make sense to her, even if none of this is fair to her.

"Stop it. I insist," I say, waving his wallet away. "If it wasn't for you, I would've laid on that football field while the football players debated on the best way to kill me."

Jake's staring at us as hard as Rafa, once again, breaks the tension. "Well, if you're buying, add my onion rings on there. Please and thank you," he says and nods at Frankie to order.

Rafa saves the day.

Aubrey leans in, her voice lowered as she requests a vanilla shake, and I feel a surge of irritation within me. Why is she here, and why am I buying her a shake? Is she trying to date Frankie? My territorial instincts kick in, and I want to make her go away somehow, even though she's not doing anything wrong.

As Frankie completes his order and firmly rejects my offer to pay by placing a ten-dollar bill on the counter, the distinctive noise of my brother's truck catches my attention. I'm almost certain his muffler fell off at least a year ago, yet he seems to relish in the fact that it now produces a sound like that of several motorcycles revving at once. On more than one occasion the neighbors have complained to my parents about it.

When he finally parks the intrusive hunk of metal invading all our ears, I witness the most disturbing thing I've seen since I swung back in time. I freeze and a chill comes over my body from my head to my toes.

Jojo's smiling and helping a girl down from his passenger side, and it's not Justine. It's Samantha Winter, and he's looking at her like he looks at Justine. What the hell is going on?

My stomach drops.

CARRIE BEAMER

Chapter Eighteen

Rafa turns to look at what seems to be distracting me. "Earth to Dessy." He snaps his fingers in front of my face.

As soon as I saw my brother's truck pulling in, my initial reaction was to wonder why Jojo would be at Pete's, seeing as he isn't allowed to eat this fast food crap. I can't believe my crazy thoughts went immediately to his previous approved food list.

Feeling unsettled, I look back and notice Jake returning Frankie's change to him and sliding the drink tray in our direction.

As I turn away, Jake gives me a creepy wink.

I nod to the parking lot and whisper to Rafa. "What the hell is my brother doing with Samantha Winter?"

"Um, dating her," he says, like it's not the Earth-shattering travesty I see it as.

I whip around to face him square on. "He's dating Justine Berry. They've been dating for years."

I look out to Jojo just as he gives Samantha a playful smack on the butt and quickly back to Rafa. The room seems to be spinning around me in a rotation of confusion. Life isn't what it's supposed to be, and it's my fault.

"*Okay*, I don't know what you're talking about, but no they haven't been dating for years, and he's also seeing Samantha. He's not serious with either one of them. I think he's playing the field like every other jock on the team." Rafa rolls his eyes with a short laugh. He isn't joking. He's being serious.

Rafa stares at what must be my distraught face and throws Aubrey and Frankie a tight-lipped smile that says we need a moment. He grabs my arm and drags me along toward the bathroom. Despite feeling a little uneasy and at risk of puking, I don't resist him and let him lead me away like a child in trouble with the teacher.

Rafa pushes the bathroom door open with one palm and kicks it shut behind us. "Something is up with you, and I need to know what it is and now. My onion rings are out there getting cold, and you're acting like a Crazy Connie over your brother," he says, grabbing both my arms and forcing me to look at him. His gentle eyes are lit up with a peaceful glint that conveys a sense of empathy and concern along with slight irritation.

I can't think straight. "He can't cheat on Justine. He would never do that," I say, with tears threating to spill down my cheeks.

"Des, what are you talking about? She knows he's seeing Samantha, because we all do. He isn't sneaking around cheating on anyone. This isn't a big deal. You knew this yesterday, so why are you being completely irrational about it today? He isn't serious with Justine."

"Yes, he is. She's practically family, or she will be." I swipe a tear away and try to control my breathing.

"She will be? Dessy, what is going on with you? You aren't making any sense. Do you know something about Justine that I don't? You don't even mention her that much, and now she's family? I've never even seen her at your house." He stretches his hand out and touches my forehead. "Are you getting a fever? You don't look well, and I can't understand why you're so upset."

"There's something you don't know, and I'm not sure how to tell you or if I can tell you. Or if I should. Maybe it's not allowed." I start crying hard now, and Rafa leans back against the door so nobody can walk in on my meltdown. This whole situation has overwhelmed me to the point that I might sit down right here and have a complete nervous breakdown, as if I didn't have one just last night in my bedroom. I'm not handling this whole life redo well at all.

"No, no, no, we're not having a bathroom breakdown at Pete's. That's it. I'm walking you home, and we're going to sort this whole mess out." He yanks me up by both arms as I try to sit down.

"But I can't abandon Frankie," I say.

"Girl, Frankie barely knows you, and he's eating with Audrey." He's done playing nice about Frankie and Aubrey. He's giving me the reality check I need.

"It's Aubrey. Her name is Aubrey, not Audrey." I wrap my arms around my own waist.

"What? You know what I don't care what her name is. She knows you about as well as Frankie, so it doesn't matter."

The truth in his words hit me like a punch in the gut, and I cry even harder. My Frankie doesn't even know me, and it's all because of my choice to save Jojo, who is currently rubbing all over Samantha Winter.

"Oh my God, Raf. I've lost him, haven't I?" I start hyperventilating.

"Oh hell, we gotta go," he says. He swiftly grabs the sunglasses dangling from his shirt and places them gently over my eyes, aiming to conceal the increasing redness and swelling. His plan is to escort me out of this place without attention. He takes a deep inhale with his eyes closed and blows it out before he opens the bathroom door. Apparently, I'm sending him over the edge, too.

He cautiously peeks out of the bathroom—like a toddler escaping from time out—to make sure no one is around, before quickly pulling me out and leading me down the hallway. We move so quickly to the side of the restaurant that no one notices us exiting and heading toward the parking lot.

As I glance back, I see Frankie taking a sip from Aubrey's vanilla shake, completely unaware that we're leaving. "Oh my God. They're sharing a shake," I say.

Rafa turns to look back.

"Frankie hates vanilla, and he's drinking after Aubrey. Are you kidding me?"

Shaking his head and walking faster, he says, "I've told you a million times drugs and or alcohol will ruin your life. You've obviously managed to ignore me and took something, because you've lost your damn mind," he says, while literally dragging me away from the restaurant to the sidewalk where we can't be seen by anyone at Pete's.

We come to a halt underneath the sprawling branches of a colossal oak tree, and I immediately double over, placing my hands on my knees, resembling a marathon runner who has just crossed the finish line. I feel like I'm on the verge of losing my mind in a way I can't come back from.

Rafa massages my back tenderly as he searches my face for a solution to my apparent breakdown. I hate that I've scared him like this. I'm his only family—that we know of right now—and the look on his face is fear. He's afraid for me, and I need to fix it.

"You know I wouldn't do drugs, and where the hell would I get alcohol? My parents don't even drink. Well, my dad has one glass of wine on Christmas and giggles all night and that's about it. I can't handle this on my own anymore. I need to confide in you about what's happening, but I don't know how to convince you to believe me," I admit, feeling overwhelmed. I rise to my feet and hastily wipe away my tears.

"Nothing you could ever say would make me think you're lying." He reassures me as he continues to comfort me by rubbing my back, but I see his right eye twitching with anxiety now as he questions what I'm going to say.

We walk in the direction of my house. I can feel his hand holding on to me tightly as I'm still quite unstable. It's as though he's afraid to let me go. His touch brings me a sense of security. I guess that's what friends do.

"It's not that you'll think I'm lying. You'll think I'm nuts."

"We've already gone there." He laughs, trying to lighten the mood, but stops when he sees I can't even muster a smile. "You know what the worst part about the whole Pete's mess is?" he asks me.

"What?"

"I forgot to get my damn onion rings." He's genuinely upset about it. Pete's onion rings are an obsession of his. You gotta love a guy who's addicted to music and onion rings.

This does make me smile—finally.

As we make our way back home, Rafa sings a new tune he's been working on for the school musical, Bring Back Birdie. I remember when he performed in that musical, and it takes me back. Strange to know I will see him do it again. The sound of his voice and the sweet, smooth melody that accompanies it has a calming effect on me. Listening to him sing is a Band-Aid for my broken heart, and I cherish every note. It's in this moment that I realize how much I've missed him. I look at him and squeeze his arm.

He nods, a smile still on his face with the realization that he's helped me calm down.

It's time to see if the universe will punish me for showing Rafa my power.

I can't do this alone anymore.

CARRIE BEAMER

Chapter Nineteen

As we reach my house, I come to a halt on the driveway and take a moment to absorb my surroundings. In the midst of my frantic state, I haven't had the chance to truly acknowledge all the things that I know, without a doubt, will change and it's all hitting me today. My mom's newly planted bushes, especially the ones I remember will die, catch my attention. I have a fleeting thought that maybe I can save them from flower death since I now know they'll get overwatered by our downspout.

Mrs. Allagash marches past me and Rafa with several white plastic Avon bags looped over both arms. She's out delivering all the neighborhood orders. She cracks me up strutting down the street in full makeup like a woman on a mission. I guess she must be modeling her products because her lipstick is so popping, I can see the bright coral from three houses away. I do know that she will continue to do this even four years from now. If you needed a good Avon lady, Mrs. Allagash is your gal.

Looking next door at the Strand's house with the knowledge that Mrs. Strand will soon have a debilitating stroke while standing in her kitchen enjoying a scoop of the jamoca almond fudge ice cream that Mr. Strand always brings her on his way home from work makes my heart splinter.

She once told me that every Monday, starting when their children were small, Mr. Strand would stop by Baskin-Robbins to get her a tub of the creamy, fudgy coffee ice cream because he knew a couple bites of that ice cream a day would help her get through the challenges of raising three small children at home.

It's an act of love that speaks volumes and shows

the depth of their commitment to each other, and it's exactly what I consider to be true love. The Strands are the real deal, much like my own parents.

Glancing at her car, it dawns on me that it will remain immobile for years to come. A sudden wave of worry washes over me, causing beads of cold sweat to form on my back. I need to tell someone, but who? Even if I did manage to muster the courage to seek help for the stroke I know is coming, I'm plagued by doubts as to whether anyone would take my concerns seriously. What do I know? I'm just a teenage kid. Or if I do tell someone and when her stroke does happen, they'll think I am a freak and probably study me in some lab. And who would blame them?

As I contemplate the inescapable reality of the situation at hand, my thoughts drift toward the many events that are destined to unfold in my neighborhood, both good and bad. The weight of these impending happenings bears down on me, and I'm overwhelmed by the magnitude of it all. I feel a sense of responsibility to address it, but I'm forced to come to terms with the fact that it's simply too much for me to handle alone. The sheer enormity of it leaves me feeling as if I've aged a hundred years in a single day. Aches and pains wrack my body as the intensity of my fear takes its toll.

If only there were a way to undo the all-consuming sense of dread that has plagued me every minute since I returned to this time in my life. It's as though, the moment I arrived, a weighty burden was placed upon my chest, making it impossible for me to draw a deep breath or find any semblance of relaxation.

I traded my worry about what would happen to Jojo and his future for everything else.

As I make my way through the front door with Rafa mumbling behind me, a sense of eerie silence descends upon me, amplified by the fact that my parents are working late at the shop and Jojo's still at Pete's with Samantha for God's sake. The familiar sight of Justine occupying the kitchen or lounging on the couch with her nursing school homework sprawled across the coffee table is no longer a part of our everyday life. The absence of Justine makes the atmosphere in my house unfamiliar and somewhat unsettling.

My mind wanders. I can't help but wonder if she's at home at this very moment, enduring the unbearable weight of her strained familial situation with her unstable dad. The mere thought of her going through such turmoil is enough to cause a physical ache in my stomach. Even though she's completely unaware that I know the complexities of her home life and her lack of a mother, my concern for her well-being only grows the more time passes.

Instead, the living room's empty, and somebody left the TV on this morning. The Smurfs are on. Azreal—the evil cat from the Smurfs—reminds me of Pony. A thud behind me causes me to turn to see Rafa as he stumbles to the floor, landing on his knees just as Ponyboy sleuths away. I look at Rafa and chuckle. "Get up and stop smurfing around."

He side-eyes the cartoon still blaring from the TV and squints at me.

"Why in the hell do y'all keep a cat that tries to kill everyone? I'm the idiot for tripping to avoid stepping on his little evil body. Next time that cat's a goner," he says, giving Pony an icy glare.

Cats are not Rafa's favorite. I know that's because of Pony, who is perched on the highest step of the staircase, casually grooming himself with his tongue. He's making long, slow strokes down his front leg as if he's completely innocent of any wrongdoing. His mischievous nature is evident as he sports a sly grin, which he nonchalantly flashes in our direction. For some reason, we can't help but feel a strange fondness for this small yet obnoxious creature. It's almost as if we're all under his spell.

"Raf?"

"Yeah?" he says, looking around as if we're waiting for something to happen because he's not sure why we're not headed up to my room yet.

"I'm about to blow your mind. Prepare yourself for me to hand you the strangest thing you've ever heard."

Taking a deep breath to prepare myself, I ascend the stairs, stepping over Pony and making my way toward my bedroom. It's next door to Jojo's room, which was formerly known as Jojo's infamous chamber of despair and desolation. Oh, how so much has changed in less than a week.

Moving down the hall, I lay my eyes on the familiar sight of the old wallpaper my mother painstakingly put up. It's adorned with a plethora of vibrant orange and avocado-colored flowers. A wave of nostalgia washes over me. Despite its outdated appearance, I can't help but feel a twinge of longing for the past for the hundredth time today. In contrast, the future wallpaper that is currently in the process of being installed appears to be nothing more than a mundane pattern of tan triangles that, upon closer inspection, are revealed to be minuscule flowers arranged in a triangular formation. The dullness of the new addition to the hall that my mom was getting ready to put up in the future seems to further highlight the stark contrast between the past and present decor.

Seeing the old bright wallpaper again makes me feel weird. It's a reminder of what I've done to my life by coming back. I can't get away from all the reminders that I shouldn't be here and that this all already happened in my life. It's a creepy feeling, and I need Rafa to know what I'm going through. I don't keep things from him, and so it's time to get it all out.

"Nobody blows my mind. I'm a ward of the state with no parents, remember? I'm immune to shock at this point. I'm clearly unfazed by the unpredictability of life thanks to mine being a mess of epic proportion." He gives a snicker with a sense of nonchalance—he's not wrong. It would take me coming from the future to blow the mind of a kid who had a turbulent childhood fraught with instability, including being shuffled between numerous foster homes since the tender age of six.

And then it hits me. Why didn't I think of this sooner? There might be only one way to convince Rafa of my claims about being from the future—by disclosing the existence of his aunt who lives in California. As I process the implications of telling Rafa about his newfound familial connection, a sudden wave of conflicting emotions washes over me.

On the one hand, the mere thought of losing Rafa once again, and perhaps even sooner than I had before, is almost too much to bear during this time of need, causing my knees to buckle involuntarily under the weight of this realization. I lean against the wall to catch myself. He's the only thing keeping me sane right now.

On the other hand, a sense of euphoria and anticipation courses through me as I think about the prospect of Rafa finally having a family to call his own after years of having no family ties. The two emotions collide and coexist within me, creating tumultuous inner thoughts I'm struggling to navigate as I come to terms with this life-altering revelation.

I shake away the thought of keeping this to

myself. I refuse to let my selfishness take over. Instead, I let my heart be filled with joy at the knowledge that I'm going to reunite him with his aunt way before he did the first time. I can no longer let him live a life deprived of a relative that will love him. He's not going to live out his high school years with me, but he won't have to do it in a foster home. That's all that matters, even if I feel torn in two over it. Not only have I lost Frankie, but I'm also going to lose Rafa too.

He plops down on my bed with a curious but concerned look on his face as I begin my pacing once again this week. I'm going to end up wearing a path down on my bedroom carpet if I don't get a grip. I obviously know his aunt's phone number, but what if she doesn't live there yet? It's technically two years ahead of schedule for Rafa to meet her. And if she does live there and answers the phone, how will I explain to her that we found her instead of the other way around like before? The emotional meeting between Rafa and his aunt was so special before, and I'm going to ruin that by doing this over the phone. Okay, who cares, it won't matter.

Casting a furtive glance at my alarm clock, I notice that the time has passed the seven o'clock threshold, marking the onset of the period when long-distance phone calls are charged at a lower rate. At least we have this going for us, because this phone call will probably be a long one.

"What in the Marching Molly are you doing? Marching back and forth in your room mumbling to yourself is not convincing me of anything apart from the fact that you might need a therapist. I'm at a loss for what's going on. I can't help with whatever this is if you don't fill me in," he says, as he motions to me and all around my room in exasperation.

"Frankie's mom is a therapist," I say, without

thinking.

"She's what? How do you know that? Oh Lord, have you been stalking him or something? I can't even handle you right now."

I barely register what he's saying as I work everything out in my mind.

He stands and grabs me by the shoulders to stop me. "*Dessy*, stop." He halts me in my place.

With my gaze locked onto Rafa's entrancing caramel-colored eyes, I reach out and clasp his face tenderly with both hands, my emotions threatening to overwhelm me as tears blur my vision. In this intimate moment, I'm acutely aware of the enormity of what's at stake, and the gravity of the decision that lies ahead. Despite the uncertainty and trepidation that grips me, I'm resolved to see this through. I know we share an unspoken understanding, a bond forged through friendship and trust. And it's this bond that gives me the courage to push forward, no matter what lies ahead.

"What is it, Des? Tell me, what's wrong?"

I immediately take his hands, guiding him to sit down right there on the floor in the center of my bedroom like we are about to perform a séance. It nearly causes Pony to be crushed in the process—he totally deserves a good ass smashing. Sitting with our legs crossed and knees touching, I lean as close as I can get to him without actually touching faces. This is a pivotal moment that requires a clear mind and steady nerves. "I'm here from the future."

Rafa's brows furrow, his face contorting in confusion as he leans back slightly, trying to get a better look at me.

My initial impulse is to close the distance between us. I stay where I am, giving him the space he needs to process his emotions and thoughts at what I just revealed.

"Oh lord lady, I need to call 9-1-1, because you have lost it. Lost *it*." He tries to stand, but I pull him back down.

"Raphael Joseph Harris, you have an aunt, and she lives in California," I say, my words hanging in the air between us. "She's your mother's sister, and she never knew about you."

As the realization dawns on him, Rafa gasps, his hand instinctively moving to his chest in shock and disbelief. I watch as his face transforms, his expression going from confusion to surprise to hope in a matter of seconds. It's as if a light has been switched on inside him, illuminating all the possibilities that exist beyond the confines of his current reality. And as I witness this transformation taking place, I can't help but feel a sense of pride, knowing I have played a small part in making it happen.

"Don't play with me, girl." He narrows his eyes and then widens them again as he knows without a shadow of doubt that I'd never make a joke or false claim about him having family.

During our sophomore year in high school, on a Father's Day, my mom invited Rafa to stay over for a cookout with our family. Earlier that day, I had spent hours helping Rafa in perfecting his audition for Starlight Theatre, a popular theater in Kansas City that hosted outdoor shows throughout the summer. He was vying for a significant role in the musical "Hair". After dinner, he performed some of the musical's songs for my parents. They, like everyone else who heard Rafa sing, were captivated by his beautiful voice.

I'll never forget that night because just as he was about to step off my driveway on his way home, he turned to me with tears rolling down his cheeks and told me that he remembered his dad visiting his mom's apartment when she was sick. Rafa's dad was dressed in bell-bottoms and a yellow turtleneck, and he was singing the same song Rafa had just learned for Hair.

The tune was low and melodious, and he had never heard it before, but he instantly recognized it when he came across it on the audition application. He was only six years old at the time and remembered only bits and pieces of the visit, but he would never forget the sound of his dad's voice. He knew it was his dad because he remembers his mom telling him to say hello to his son. He had never told anyone about the only day he ever saw his dad until that moment on my driveway.

Ready to bring it all home, I gently grasp Rafa's hands with mine and tell him that in the future, he'll be able to tell me all about the man in the yellow turtleneck singing the beautiful melody from the musical Hair. Tears well up in his eyes, and his hands start trembling as he looks up, searching for the memory of the song. It's evident he's trying to recall which song it could be as he hasn't auditioned for this musical yet, and I feel his palms growing clammy in my grip.

"Look up the musical Hair. You'll recognize it when you hear it."

In that moment, a sudden spark ignites in his eyes again. He takes in a sharp breath, his hand immediately rising to his throat in shock. He remembers his dad visiting, and knows he's never told anyone. He believes me. How could he not? I can see the goosebumps erupt all over his arms.

I spend the next hour telling Rafa why I came back. I don't go into the swing details and all of that. I think I should probably keep some of this a secret or at least my portal vessel should stay unknown. I tell him what happens to Jojo and his jaw drops. He stops me for a minute so he can take in what I've said so far. This is a lot to process, and he wants to make sure he doesn't miss anything. When he tries to interrupt, I tell him to hold all questions until I'm done.

The best part is explaining how he ends up relocating to live with his aunt in California. I tell him that I met her—in the future—and she's a loving, wonderful person who was overjoyed to discover her sister had a child, despite being devastated by her sister's passing.

As I speak, a curious mixture of emotions seems to be overwhelming him, causing him to both weep with sorrow and applaud with joy. I see a bit of hesitation on his face, like maybe this is too good to be true, like he's dreaming.

Bringing him up to speed on Jojo and Justine—and me and Frankie—makes me feel nauseous.

When he finally puts the whole Frankie meltdown from Pete's together, he lets out a loud, "*Oh*."

"He's the love of my life, Raf, and I've lost him."

He wipes the tears from my face I didn't realize were falling again and then wipes his own with the back of his sleeve.

I hop up and drag my phone down to the floor, parking it between us. "I know your Aunt Kristi's number because I obviously call you a lot in the future." I huff out a breath. I'm talking too fast. I see him mouth the name 'Kristi' over and over for a couple of seconds. "Now how do we explain all of this to your aunt?" I say.

He's staring at the ceiling, zoning out.

"Rafa?"

He wraps his arms around himself and begins crying again.

I scoot next to him. "I know this is a lot."

He nods and wipes his face.

"You deserve this. And trust me, you love

California." I laugh because Rafa and I have always known that the Midwest is not his jam.

"Thank you, Dessy, thank you. How can I ever repay you?" Then he tilts his head sideways and says, "And, girl … you've been through it! How are you holding up? I was starting to think you were having a complete mental breakdown."

"Um, I totally am." I laugh and shake my head. I have no words for how this chaos feels, but it's going to be so much easier to handle now that Rafa knows what's going on. "First, let's call your aunt and tell her she has the most amazing and incredible nephew stuck out here in Missouri."

"Damn straight she does." He snaps his fingers and gives me a high five.

Then I say what I know he was just wondering about, because I wondered about it too. I place my hand on top of his as it rests on the phone. "And, Raf? I can't go back to a time when I didn't know you."

He lifts his chin up and blinks the last of his tears away with a look of acknowledgement.

I can't go back and save his mother from dying. I haven't tried it, but I know that without knowing Rafa when he was little, I can't conjure up a memory to go back to.

I truly can't imagine going back to age six. The idea of having to relearn the recorder in my elementary music class or endure those repugnant, pink sponge curlers my mother twisted my hair into every evening is utterly unbearable. Those curlers left deep indentations in my scalp that I could feel all day long while sitting at my desk in class looking like Shirley Temple. Just thinking about it makes me wince. But I would love to go back to a good old scholastic book fair. The anticipation of going down to the library with money in my pocket and the promise of coming home with a poster and new book always brought about so much happiness. I think I still have the Bugs Bunny poster, featuring him sitting in a sports car, rolled up in my closet somewhere.

Bookfairs were the best.

Chapter Twenty

Rafa decides to just wing it. When he dials the number I have for his aunt, she answers on the third ring. He decides not to waste any time contemplating what to say or devising a plausible tale about how he learned of her existence—we certainly couldn't reveal the truth.

While he begins speaking, he grabs his right wrist with two fingers from his left hand and checks his pulse. This is something we learned to do in gym class. Rafa seems to think seeing how fast your heart is beating at and any given time is fun, because he does it a lot. I bet his heartrate is through the roof right now.

"Hi, I'm Rafa. My mother Janelle died when I was six, and I'm pretty sure I'm your nephew." His voice quivers at first, but gradually grows steadier over time. It is evident by his excitement and waving hands that they click immediately, almost as if they have known each other for years.

This rapid connection between them is incredibly heartening, and I'm delighted to see that things are happening in the same way they did before. Well ... almost.

Finally, amidst the chaos and confusion of returning to the past, something positive has emerged, aside from Jojo not getting injured that is. I observe him as he talks with so much enthusiasm, and I can't help but notice the remarkable transformation that has taken place within minutes. Before this phone call, he sat on my bedroom floor with his shoulders hunched over like a drooping flower desperately thirsting for water and sunlight. As the conversation goes on, he grows taller and begins to blossom and flourish. Now, he's sitting up straight, with an expression of unbridled joy that I bet won't leave his face anytime soon, if ever.

Through the rest of the phone conversation, I selfishly think about Frankie while I see the day turning to evening through my bedroom window. With the stars realigning themselves for Rafa, I feel as if I can go back to my mission of winning Frankie back. The persistent ache of uncertainty regarding Jojo and Justine continues plaguing me, and it feels as if a tight rubber band is constricting my chest. I fear if this tension continues building, I may eventually snap under the pressure.

I can't get past my brother's betrayal. Okay, it's not really betrayal based off the fact that he and Justine were together in the future and that hasn't happened yet, but still, I feel what I feel. I need to figure out what to do to convince Jojo to be done with Samantha and concentrate on Justine. Justine needs us. She needs my family.

She hasn't started working at my parent's shop yet. That didn't happen until after Jojo's injury. Why are we even in this situation? These girls need to make him choose. I wouldn't stand for anyone dating me and someone else. It's like Jojo thinks he's God's gift to the world. I forgot that before his accident, he was never home. Is this really who he was, and I just wasn't paying attention to what a selfish flirt he was?

Here I was thinking my biggest problem would be how to rekindle Frankie's love for me. I'd not seen this mess of Justine coming at me. I feel responsible for her somehow—she's family to me now. I'm left wondering if fate will bring Jojo and Justine together naturally or if Samantha will successfully win him over, causing him to forget about Justine entirely. This never would've happened if I left Jojo injured instead of trying to come back here and fix it.

Justine losing Jojo like I lost Frankie was not part

of the plan, but my brother's health had to come before any of it—accepting it is another story.

Maybe I need to take a step back and let the situation play out for a few weeks, but the thought of doing that makes me anxious. My mind has become accustomed to continuously working toward aligning the future I came from, and the mere idea of pausing for even a minute causes my thoughts to unravel like a pile of shredded cheese.

If my power works like it did in the future, I think I can see how things go for two weeks and then swing back to now if I need to. I will have to swing away two weeks if Jojo doesn't realize he needs to be with Justine and he gets closer to Samantha, but at least I have the option. God, this is a mess and swinging back puts me continually moving in reverse, not getting these next four years over with and back to my senior year of high school. Swinging back and forth once I came back wasn't something I even considered before, but it would be dumb not to at least use what I have, I guess. I know one thing—I'm never doing this day over again.

Rafa grabs my attention and gestures wildly with his hands, as if he is drawing on imaginary paper with an invisible pen.

"Oh, you need a paper and pen?" I scramble to go dig through my schoolbag.

He rolls his eyes at me like, duh.

From what I'm hearing, it appears that Rafa's aunt, who happens to be a lawyer, is going to schedule to fly in this week to meet him and initiate the legal paperwork and process to take custody of him. In the past, I recall her efficiently managing the whole transfer of Rafa to her when she arrived in Missouri without any hiccups. It's all going to happen so fast—he'll be gone in a month.

With an anxious expression, he gestures toward my alarm clock and flashes an uneasy smile, mouthing the words "I'm sorry'. This call is going to cost me some money, and he knows it. My parents made me work off my long-distance calls to Rafa at their shop before.

I dismiss his concern with a wave of my hand, but he still holds onto my hand and continues to nod and speak. It's only a single phone call, and I'm confident my mom will be thrilled for Rafa once she discovers the reason behind it. I've heard my parents in their room at night talking through adopting Rafa, and I never told him about it. I didn't want to get his hopes up if it wasn't going to happen. To be honest, I think they were getting ready to pull the trigger and start doing something about it when we found out about Rafa's aunt.

As I hear my parents come in downstairs, the wreath my dad crafted for my mom a couple of Halloweens ago emits a disturbing meow and a blood curdling scream. The wreath, decorated with black and orange ribbon and covered in spooky black cats, features a sound contraption that produces a fake creepy cat's meow. This sound is so unsettling it causes Ponyboy's fur to stand on end, and he jumps up in fright every single time. I've seen him jump a foot in the air it rattles him so much. Whenever any of us observe Pony's reaction, it never fails to make us laugh. I wonder where that wreath went. I remember the wreath being on display for a few years, remaining on our front door throughout the year, even during Christmas. It wasn't because my parents were overly enthusiastic about Halloween and wanted decorations up year-round, but because we loved seeing Pony's hilarious response to it.

Suddenly it hits me. Maybe this is why Pony is so mean—what a thought after all this time. It's a feline payback! I gotta throw that wreath out asap. I can at least save him another year of torture.

Rafa begins wrapping up his call.

"Des?" My mom yells from the bottom of the stairs, and I remember it's my night to cook dinner. This is their late night at the shop. I was just going to throw a frozen pizza in the oven, but I forgot all about it.

"Coming in a sec," I yell as I dump my school bag on my carpet and scatter my books and folders in all directions. I'm going to tell them I was engrossed in my homework with Rafa, and the time got away from us. I'm not ready to fill them in on Rafa and California. The events of the day have been too overwhelming, and I need a break from any further explanations of anything right now. I feel utterly exhausted from it all.

"Now that's a phone call I never dreamed I'd have." Rafa hangs up with a whimsical grin on his face.

"Well, you're definitely not dreaming. I'll tell you one thing for sure—we couldn't make up this whole craziness if we tried."

Both of us stare at each other with wide-eye amazement.

"Hi, I'm from the future, and you're moving to California to live with a long-lost aunt," he says in a high-pitched voice, mocking me from earlier, fake flipping his hair.

We collapse onto the floor, erupting in fits of laughter.

"Des, this is truly wild. Wild!" He slaps the ground and raises his fist in victory. He turns toward me. "Before I move, we have some work to do."

"We do?" I look over at him with our arms and legs entangled on the floor of my bedroom.

"Hell yes. Girl, we gotta get you Frankie back!"

I hug him so tightly he lets out a squeal. Thank God I have him to lean on now with this time travel nightmare. It's clear that doing this without him was unraveling me.

He sits up, his jaw tightening, and a look of intense focus takes over his face as he begins preparing with a maniacal determination. "Prepare yourself, Des, because we're about to unleash all the magic we have. We have to use what you already know about Frankie and make it seem legit but also not stalker freaky. You know what I'm saying? Weave it into situations that'll have him looking at you like he knows you on a deeper level. We want to draw him in to what he fell in love with in the first place."

He's nodding and smiling. He then belts out *It's My Turn* by Diana Ross.

My heart aches at the thought of not being with Rafa like this for much longer. Thank God for the phone calls that'll keep us connected. Even though it means working extra at my parents' shop, I'll do whatever it takes to pay the phone bills from the countless long-distance calls I'm going to be making. I can't imagine going a day without his guidance, and I'll need it more than ever now.

As my mom walks into the room, she lets out a sigh of pure joy with a huge smile from ear to ear. The sound of Rafa's voice has the uncanny ability to calm any irritation or frustration you might feel with the world in a single moment. His voice has the power to envelop you in a blanket of peace and tranquility, leaving you feeling renewed and restored. I can feel the goosebumps on my arms now, and a deep sense of calm that washes over me. I'm so very thankful for my Rafa.

Chapter Twenty-One

I sleep better than I have in the days since I swung back.

Rafa, who's waiting for his Aunt Kristi's arrival this week, is busy deciphering what we think is Frankie's class schedule. I obviously knew his schedule before, but I assume it's changed since mine and Rafa's are jumbled up.

I told Rafa about the schedules changing, and he wanted to know if he liked his schedule the first time because he hates it now. I told him the only class he liked before was choir, and that was never changing, to which he agreed. We still have lunch together now, so I see that as a win, even though Frankie isn't in there with us like before.

The plan is to run into Frankie in the hallway, locate his after-school hangout spot, and covertly observe Aubrey's behavior to gauge the seriousness of her relationship with Frankie. My aim is to find a way to insert myself into their social circle without appearing overbearing, irrational, or just plain weird. Right now, I'm all of those things.

If he'd started working at Dunkin' Donuts before we began dating, I'd have found a way to visit him there. But he didn't start until about six months later, so I can't casually bump into him at a job he doesn't have yet. I obviously know where he lives, but it's about a twenty-minute walk so casually cruising by his house would be stalkerish. Rafa would never go for it.

I decide to set my alarm an hour earlier than my usual time, but this time it isn't to prepare Jojo's nutritious breakfast and lunch—those days are over. As the crack of dawn breaks, I hear *Jessie's Girl* by Rick

Springfield blaring from my brother's clock radio. The thud that follows as he staggers out of bed for his before school, early morning football practice is something I haven't heard in years. I feel a sense of relief and contentment, at least with regards to his physical well-being. The world around my family seemed to fall back into place, and a feeling of satisfaction fills me as I know he is off pursuing his football dreams once again.

I cozily nestle into my bed with Pony, who is perched on top of the plush, lavender cushions crafted by my mom as an eighth-grade Valentine's Day present. With eager anticipation, I snuggle deeper into my comforter, armed with a pen and a notebook to officially get started on this homework Rafa gave me. All the things I'm going to write down future Rafa already knew, and it's crazy to think that I have to refresh him on all things Frankie.

With a sense of purpose, I begin my task by skillfully sketching Frankie's name in bold, bubbly letters at the very top of the page. While I draw, I reflect on our relationship and my mind drifts, but I quickly refocus my attention, trying not to let the tears I feel coming spill over. I proceed to jot down a series of bullet points, each detailing a distinctive trait or idiosyncrasy that sets Frankie apart and makes him so special to me.

- He has a contagious laugh that's loud and cheerful but not obnoxious or grating. And he can brighten up any room.

- No matter how dull his day at school or work is, Frankie can lift any bad mood with a hilarious story or joke. He's ready to share with anyone in need of a good laugh.

- He's passionate about nursing (well he will be) and helping others out of a bind. I've witnessed him pull his jeep over to assist an elderly lady in loading her groceries into the trunk of her car. It's just in his nature to lend a helping hand whenever he sees someone in need. For him, it's not a choice, but rather an instinct that defines him as a person.

- He's not afraid to be silly and spontaneous, even in public. During a visit to the mall, we stumbled upon a section in JCPenney's that sold outrageously ugly dress clothes. Despite being there to shop for his mom's birthday present, we couldn't resist the temptation to try on the ridiculous outfits just for the fun of it. He was completely unbothered by the possibility of being seen by anyone we knew. His carefree spirit makes everything fun.

- He has a deep love for good music and kickass t-shirts, as evidenced by his daily wardrobe choice of concert tees ranging from hip hop to alternative rock. I can't remember a single day where he wasn't sporting one, except maybe for prom night. He even wears them under his mighty dogger costume.

- He has the peculiar talent of juggling various objects with ease, whether it's apples, tennis balls, bananas, or even a set of coffee mugs. He never ceases to amaze me with his impressive juggling skills.

- His contagious positivity is truly inspiring. He always manages to see the silver lining in every situation. When I fell on the field while trying to save Jojo, instead of dwelling on my clumsiness, he complimented me and made me feel like a hero. It's this very quality that makes me love him the most.

As I reminisce about countless cherished memories, a bittersweet smile creeps across my face, intermingled with the salty taste of tears that has escaped without my notice. This list could go on and on.

I write down his favorite foods, the songs we danced to at our last school dance—that haven't hit the airwaves yet—and the ways I always knew how to make him laugh. The list grows longer with every passing moment, capturing all the things that make him so special to me.

Finishing up, I read it back to myself.

When I hear my parents making their coffee and moving about in the kitchen, I know I'm running late for school.

"Des, you're gonna miss the bus ... again."

"I'm coming," I yell, scurrying around my room. Some things about my future self and past self, are very much the same—I'm never on time.

I have Rafa help wrestle my long, tangled hair into a French braid on the bus. It's funny because this is something we did before, and it's comforting to repeat something from the past while being back in the past. Mornings like this also remind me why I cut my hair short. I don't have the time or patience for long hair.

"So, I'm going to follow Frankie after English since it's my last hour and see who he meets up with after school. I don't know if he rides the bus or gets a ride from someone."

"He drives a jeep," I say, handing him a ponytail holder over my shoulder to secure my hair.

I don't know where he learned to braid, but the braid starts at the crown of my head and extends all the way down the middle of my back, giving me an air of effortless beauty. Once he moves, I'm screwed. I remember that's when I cut my hair short, after he left for California.

"He can't drive a jeep. He's only fifteen, remember?" Rafa tsks and shakes his head at me.

I slap my forehead. "Geez, this whole erasing

almost four years of your life scenario is really messing with me."

"Girl, you and me both."

As we approach the school bus line, we gather our stuff and stand up. Putting my big hoop earrings in and swiping some lip gloss over my lips, I scan the kids hurriedly piling out of buses like ants released from a glass jar. Amidst the bustle of kids rushing around, my attention is suddenly arrested by the sight of Frankie getting off the bus in front of mine, and I feel my breath catch in my throat.

As he steps off the curb onto the sidewalk, I can't help but stare in awe at his effortless swagger and the easy way he carries himself. His tousled hair and familiar features only add to my excitement at seeing him.

Rafa spots him too. "Hells bells, lady, we have to get you off this bus and now. You need to catch him when he's alone. This is your chance to make it seem like you just bumped into him." Rafa nudges all the kids in front of us. "Let's go, people. Move!"

Kids roll their eyes at his dramatic yelling.

"Hold my stuff." I shove my notebook and books on top of his and jump over every seat in front of me to get to the front.

"Okay, well that's one way to do it," I hear Rafa call after me with a snap and a chuckle.

Shannon, our bus driver, nods her head at me while I'm hurdling the bus seats like an Olympian gone wrong and says, "Cool braid." She's a total hippie and wears some sort of bandanna every day. Her bandannas are not worn in an Olivia Newton-John "I like to work out and get physical" way, but more of a Willie Nelson "I'm high and on the road again" way. She gives a small wave that conveys a casual "catch you later, man" vibe and I can't help but think she's probably one of the best bus drivers a bunch of rowdy high school kids could want.

My heart's racing as I practically fall out of the bus. Taking a deep breath and gathering myself, I summon my courage and approach Frankie, who stands on the sidewalk, completely engrossed in a piece of paper in his hand. Despite feeling somewhat unsure about what to say, I try keeping my demeanor nonchalant and not come across as a lunatic.

I greet Frankie with a hesitant "Hey." My awkwardness still lingers as I fight the urge to rush up to him and shower him with hugs and kisses. It seems like I'll never become used to this feeling. He glances up, curious to see who just greeted him because, sadly, my voice isn't familiar to him.

"Oh, hey, Dessy."

I swallow hard at hearing him say my name. "Yeah, it's actually Desirae, but yeah I go by Dessy." I don't know why I felt the need to tell him this. I feel like an idiot.

"Desirae, that's a pretty name," he says with that genuine smile of his.

I work hard keeping my emotions in check. The first time I told him my full name he said the very same thing. I'm glad he hasn't asked why I disappeared from Pete's the other night. I can't tell him I had a melt down and Rafa had to drag me home like a lost child so we could discuss that I'm a time traveler.

As the ten-minute warning bell chimes, both of us begin making our way toward the front doors of the school amidst a chaotic swarm of kids weaving in and out, rushing in all directions. Even with the frenzy around us, I try holding a conversation with him. I'm not ready to lose his attention. "So, you're the school mascot, huh? That's pretty cool."

"Yeah, I'm trying to be anyway," he says with a small laugh.

I'm struggling to think of things to say that make it seem like I don't know much about him. Suddenly, it strikes me that Frankie and I never dawdled outside the school before first period because we always came early to help Mr. Tim. Frankie made it a point to help Mr. Tim, the elderly school janitor, every morning before first period. He helped the old man carry his cleaning supplies from the janitor closet to the front of the building, unwilling to watch him struggle down the hallway alone. I'm not sure when he began this kind act—Rafa's advice rings true—I should utilize my knowledge of Frankie to impress him.

"Well, I have to hustle, I saw Mr. Tim, the janitor, struggling to get all his stuff down to the front office last week, and I want to see if he needs help before first hour."

Frankie's face lights up and an expression of affection for my wanting to help others shows in the happiness spreading across his face. He brings the best out in me. "That is such a great idea. I'll go with you."

Damn, I'm good, I think to myself as I rush off to help Mr. Tim with Frankie.

CARRIE BEAMER

Chapter Twenty-Two

As I reach my locker, Rafa's standing with his hands on his hips, tapping his foot overdramatically, so I know he's annoyed. A heap of my books surrounds his feet. He doesn't seem too pleased I left him to carry all my stuff. However, his mood quickly shifts when I tell him I'd gone to assist Mr. Tim with Frankie.

"Okay, now that's what I'm talking about. I don't know who Mr. Tim is, but you were with Frankie so that's something. You're gonna have this boy back in no time," he exclaims, with a surge of excitement.

While I try matching his confidence, I can't help but feel a bit doubtful.

"Also, I found out he eats during first lunch. You've got to position yourself around the cafeteria then." He gestures toward the cafeteria, swirling his hands in the air as he speaks.

My heart sinks. "No way I can make that happen. I have English class at the other end of the school during first lunch." I swirl my hands back at him in frustration.

He gently puts one hand on my shoulder and lowers his eyes to mine, staring at me intently until he knows he has my full attention. His eyelashes are so long and thick I used to call him Mr. Snuffleupagus from Sesame Street. I take a deep breath and allow him to calm me.

"Des, you must make the big moves. Don't you want more of what you just had with him helping Mr. Tom? Besides, anything they're doing in English you already did the first time around, so you'll figure it out. English is your jam. This is so nuts." He laughs at that thought.

"It's Mr. Tim not Tom."

"Okay?" He rolls his eyes at my correction, removing his hand from my shoulder and situating his books.

"I don't know, Raf. He was chatty, but it was friend chatty not I'm going to fall in love with you chatty." I pick up my books and prepare myself to head to first hour. Sitting in class is the last thing I want to do right now. With the impending ringing of the bell, my mind races in several directions, leaving me feeling scattered and unfocused. Not to mention I slopped mop water on my feet and now my white Keds are soggy. Frankie offered to dry them off with some of Mr. Tim's towels, but I politely declined. Of course, he offered to help me dry my shoes—he's the best human I know aside from Rafa.

"Yes, but remember you said you guys were friends for a couple of months before it all started. Right?"

"Yeah, I guess. It just felt, I don't know … different than before."

"You can't come from the future and think you'll perfectly recreate it. I can't believe I just said that." He shakes off the weirdness of it. "It's going to look different, but the outcome will be the same. The outcome is your focus."

The bell rings and we both groan.

"Now I have you making me late. Don't worry, okay? Remember it's the outcome! Just stick with the plan. We've got this." He rushes off to class mumbling to himself about being late.

How the hell am I going to do this once he's in California? I need him here.

Sitting in class, surrounded by a sea of faces I'd forgotten about until now, I'm once again struck by the weight of knowledge. I know that some of these kids will experience incredible highs and devastating lows during their high school years, and yet they have no idea what's in store for them. I'll never get used to the strangeness of knowing that.

My mind quickly turns to Frankie, and the weight of everything else fades for a minute. I replay the conversation over and over in my head that I had with Frankie this morning, and the one comforting thing about it is the fact that I didn't see Aubrey. It solidifies to me that he isn't dating her. Frankie is the type of boyfriend that walks you to your class and waits for you before school. He didn't hesitate to spend his last few minutes before class with me, and Aubrey certainly never came looking for him. A glimmer of hope shines through, and I relax a bit.

As the teacher drones on robotically like the teacher on Charlie Brown, I decide Rafa's right. I'm going to have to find a reason to bump into Frankie during first lunch. English is my best subject, so being five minutes late won't hurt anything. The thought of just talking to him again makes my heart swoon with happiness.

CARRIE BEAMER

Chapter Twenty-Three

After searching for Frankie for more than twenty minutes while trying to look like I belonged in first lunch, I finally spot him. He's sitting with some of the football players. My spirit deflates. Since they're already sitting together, I can't just approach their table. I am unsure of what to say and don't want to seem out of place. I wanted to bump into him effortlessly, which is not going to happen right now or ever again it feels like.

I admire how the football players welcome the energetic kid who runs around the field in a Mighty Dogger suit hyping everyone up. Most the guys on the team seem like conceited jerks when they come to the house with my brother. I briefly wonder what lunch shift Jojo is in, because I don't see him at the table. He better not be sitting somewhere with Samantha Winter.

The trip to the cafeteria is worth it though, because I see Aubrey and she is sitting three tables away from Frankie's. If they were together, surely he'd be sitting with her. We always sat together at lunch with Rafa. We were lucky to have the same lunch shift back then and not so lucky this time around. I'm going to count Aubrey as a small threat and not the relationship killer I envisioned she might be for me. He's not that into her, and maybe she's not that into him, although I don't know how she couldn't be. Either way I'm over the moon about this new revelation.

As I make my way to my English class, feeling better about things for a change, I catch sight of Justine entering the bathroom. Even though Justine recognizes me as Jojo's sister, we're not particularly close yet. I need to pull her back in with the Ortega family—she belongs with us. Maybe if I can get to know her better it'll help

Jojo see that she's the one for him, not Samantha. How does he not feel what he did before when he's with her? They were so close, and I believe they truly loved one another.

My plans are abruptly altered as I enter the bathroom and find her sobbing.

She's leaning against the tampon dispenser with her face buried in her hands.

I can't go for the lighthearted greeting I had originally anticipated.

She peeks at me through her fingers, like a child playing peek-a-boo, to see who came in. She inches toward one of the stalls so she can be alone. Giving me a small smile and trying to wipe her tears away like she wasn't just totally losing it, she looks like the Justine I am used to. The girl that always had a somber expression even through a smile.

"Hey, Justine."

"Hey." Her voice is a whisper.

"Are you okay? I mean, I know you're not okay, but can I do anything to help?" I move closer to her but act like I'm checking my makeup in the dirty, water splashed mirror. Just like when I used to have talks with her, she looks like she wants to bolt. I want to ask her if it's her dad and his issues that's causing this breakdown, but I'm not supposed to know about him or any of her deepest hurts and secrets.

She pauses for a second, seemingly trying to decide if she can open up to me.

I try to play it cool, so she feels less pressure. I do know Justine, and she folds under pressure.

"It's just that…" Before she can go on, she starts crying again, but this time she does go into the stall, and I hear the clank of the latch as she locks herself in.

Getting close to her is going to be harder than I

thought. It took her months to open up to me and my mom about her dad. Only one time did she even bring her mom up, causing my mom to cry and hug Justine over and over. It was a hug Justine had needed from a mother her entire life. That hug helped her decide to be a nurse and help others through any bad thing they had ailing them. It was beautiful to watch Justine blossom, and now I see that fixing my brother didn't help Justine at all.

"It's just that what, Justine? I know you don't know me that well, but you can talk to me. Us girls have to stick together. Right? Justine?"

I can hear her trying to regulate her crying behind the door by taking deep inhales and exhales. I get it—that's all I've done since I came back it seems. Now I know what Rafa has been dealing with.

"It's just that I thought your brother liked me, like really liked me."

The crying continues from behind the ugly gray bathroom door—so much for the deep calming breaths. I move closer to the stall door and see that someone wrote "Josie Jones sucks it all". Well, that's unfortunate if you're Josie Jones. I don't know her, but I'm quite sure she doesn't suck it all, whatever it all is. I make a mental note to come back here and scratch that out with a marker. I just told Justine that girls have to stick together, and I'm going to follow through on that.

"Well, he does like you, Justine. I've seen you together, and I can tell he likes you."

I have no idea if this is true, because all I've seen them do is make out. Plus, I know he likes Samantha, so I'm kind of lying but not fully. I peek between the cracks into the bathroom stall and see her just staring down at the toilet.

"If he liked me, I wouldn't have to hear from Heather Slack in third hour today that he played truth or dare Saturday night with Marianne Fremont, and they did a lot more than just make out." She blows her nose, and it sounds like the clarinet I tried playing in eighth grade. "We had a date planned, but he cancelled because he said he needed down time after the game Friday night. I should've known it was a lie. I'm so stupid."

I wait for her to finish the second round of clarinet nose blowing. "Don't say that. You're not stupid." I hate to hear anyone call themselves stupid unless it's Jake the Gigolo. He is stupid.

"You don't know me that well like you just said and yes, I am. I believed that me and Jojo had something, and it turns out we have nothing."

She's bothered about Marianne Fremont but not Samantha Winter? I don't get it. Is my brother just a big cheater and user?

"That's not true. You do have something special. Don't give up on him, Justine. I think he loves you." The minute the words are out of my mouth I know I'm in trouble. At this point, I don't know who or what my brother loves aside from football. I back away from the door, wishing I could bolt.

"He what?" She unlocks the stall and opens the door so fast I step as close to the exit I can get. She just stares at me with swollen eyes and her red tipped nose. Her mascara is doing a number on her face right now. It looks like someone ran a black marker up and down her cheeks.

I move to the sink to wet a paper towel and hand it to her.

She takes it but doesn't do anything with it. "He loves me? You heard him say that?"

She looks confused but hopeful, and it's the saddest thing ever.

"I ... well ... yeah. He said something like that to

me and my mom at dinner the other night." I swallow hard, hoping not to give away the lie. I'm in deep with this. How will I cover such a huge lie?

"What exactly did he say?" Nervously, she dabs the paper towel under her eyes, but it's gonna take a lot more effort than that to fix her makeup. She looks like she got kicked out of the band KISS.

"It was something like, I really like hanging with Justine and I think I love her."

She put her hand over her mouth in shock.

This is getting worse by the second. The more I talk, the more lies I tell. Jojo's going to murder me, and this is so wrong to do to Justine.

"Then why would he mess around with Marianne Fremont?" She's looking at me as if I can solve the world's problems right now.

"Oh, you know how guys can be. He made a mistake, a huge mistake. I'm sure he's sorry. Or maybe it's a rumor? I bet Heather Slack was mistaken, and it was someone else. The rumor mill at this school grows stronger every day, especially with the football players. I mean Josie Jones is being accused of sucking it all. Nobody sucks it all." I'm rambling and can't seem to stop.

This is not me. If she were one of my friends or anyone else to be honest, I'd tell her that what he did was wrong. I'd say that he's a total scumbag and he deserves to be called out for his despicable behavior. I'd tell her she needs to rid her life of him and not look back. I'm just so desperate for her and Jojo to be what they were that I'm giving the worst advice anyone could give in this situation.

"You know what, Justine, I'm going to talk to him for you. I'll get to the bottom of this. Maybe this is all just a big misunderstanding." Although from what I've seen out of my brother lately, I'm guessing it's all true. Jojo has become the type of guy I can't stand and I'm beyond disappointed.

"You'd do that for me?"

"Of course. I think you guys could have something cool together."

"Really?" She finally cracks a small smile for false reasons.

"Yeah. I know my brother, and you seem nice. That's just what he needs."

I wish I wouldn't have said that last part. Nobody should be just what someone needs.

The bell rings and I realize I just missed my entire English class as well as my own lunch shift. This day has officially gone to hell and for the first time since I swung back here, I'm going to have to swing back again, to Saturday so I can stop Jojo from doing whatever the hell he did with Marianne Fremont.

I'm going to tell Rafa what's happened so he can at least know I have to go through this whole bathroom meet up again with Justine. I need someone to know what the hell I'm going through. This time though, I'm going to put some safeguards in place so Rafa knows when I swung back and when we're starting again.

I'm a complete mess.

Chapter Twenty-Four

I am completely drained from recounting the entire ordeal to Rafa during our bus ride home. He can't understand why I feel so strongly about Jojo and Justine. If he could remember how they were before he'd get it.

"Des, you gave your brother his football back. You can't save his relationship and yours at the same time. You need to focus your efforts on Frankie. That's the relationship that needs to be on your mind and only that one. If Jojo messes up his chance with Justine, that's his business. You can't go around being a Save Everyone Sally."

He undoes my hair and brushes it out in long strokes. The spindles on the brush gliding down my back relaxes me. That braid from this morning was giving me a headache on top of all the other day's events.

"She doesn't have any family. I told you about her dad. Her home life's a nightmare. She needs my family. She needs my mom. You should understand that more than anyone, Raf."

"What I understand is that you need to wash this hair. You can't worry yourself about it. If she needs family, then become friends with her. You're going to need someone here that you know you can trust once I move. That'll solve the problem of her not being with your family and alleviate the loneliness you'll feel once I'm gone. I mean she won't replace me, obviously. I'm fabulous and totally irreplaceable." He laughs, handing me back my brush, knowing this is true.

I take a moment to consider the idea. The notion of her and Jojo not being together feels so unfamiliar and wrong, but I genuinely like her as a friend when she's not spoiling my brother with unhealthy snacks and soda, which has fortunately been resolved. It'd be comforting to have her at the house again. I'm confident my mom and her can re-establish their previous level of closeness and bond. Justine fit into our family like butter goes with toast. The issue is Jojo.

"I don't know if that'll work. I can tell she's already in love with my brother. I think her being around him would be too hard for her and make it awkward."

"You need to make it work. Tell her how disgusting he is. That shouldn't be hard because he's kind of being a jerk these days. Sorry, but he is. Make her see him differently and see you as one of the best friends she never knew she needed. Maybe someday it'll happen naturally for them, but at least it gets her out of her house and with your family most of the time."

I can see what he's saying. If I'm gonna let Jojo get away with his sordid truth or dare shenanigans, then all I need to do is swing back to before I told her all that nonsense about him loving her and how she shouldn't give up. I'll go back to the bathroom and tell her he's not worthy of her and she should make him experience the pain of being rejected by someone as amazing as herself. This is what I wished I would've said anyway.

I just need to find a way to help her believe in herself and be strong where Jojo's concerned. Honestly, I don't get all the hype over my brother. I guess sisters don't see what other girls see in their brothers. He's just a smelly guy I hear fart in the bathroom every morning. He's not a cute boy you'd want to swoon over. Sisters know too much.

"You're my life saver, Raf."

"Duh."

"I have to go back in time to first lunch so I can meet her in the bathroom again. I need to talk her out of wanting to be with him but win her over, so she wants to hang out with me. Who wouldn't want to hang out with me?"

With so much confidence in this new idea, I embrace Rafa in a tight, hug but he resists my hug and forces me to look at him.

"What do you mean go back? You can go back? Again?"

"Yeah, I think so. I used to do it all the time before. I'd go back two times in a day sometimes. Life got very complicated, especially with you in California."

He looks around us and leans into me. "I can't have conversations with you thinking I've already had them. This madness scares me. Like have we already done this bus ride before? I mean, was Shannon wearing those rainbow overalls before too?"

He motions toward the bus driver, who's in paint-striped denim overalls that have concert buttons pinned all the way down the straps.

I can tell he's genuinely spooked at this thought. It does seem like witchcraft.

"What? No. I would tell you if I was going back. But since I am going back, I need to give you a sign or something, so you know I went back. Maybe you won't get so spooked about it that way?"

He looks around the bus like the whole thought of it scares him to even imagine.

"I know you want to keep how you go back a secret. That's fine. I don't even want to know, but, girl, if you're going back, you might as well go back to your time with Frankie and Mr. Tom this morning. Make it more memorable this time."

"It's Tim, and you're a damn genius, Raf." I lean in and hug him even tighter.

"Again, duh. Enough with all the hugging. Shannon keeps staring at us through her mirror as if we're the ones who look bizarre right now."

I look up at Shannon, and she gives us a thumbs up over her head, smiling into the giant rearview mirror. She's not even watching the road through her oversized sunglasses.

"Give me your notebook."

He pulls it out from between two books and a note falls onto his lap. "Oh, here, I wrote you a note sixth hour because we watched a film on The Great Depression, and I was feeling depressed enough."

"I've watched that one in Mr. Nyquist's class. I agree it's brutal to watch." I take the note, shoving it in my pocket so I can read it later, and grab a pen from my purse. "I'm gonna write on the back of your notebook, and we're both going to sign it so we can keep track of all this madness."

He nods in agreement.

I write the date and time it is now and the date and time I'm going back to. We both sign underneath it. "So, when I see you again on the bus—I need you to redo my hair or else I would just swing back to seeing Frankie outside the school—I'll ask for your notebook and circle the date and time we are presently at, which will be this one." I point to the spot on the notebook that said 7:15 AM with today's date.

"This will help me keep track, but I really hope you're not going to make a habit of this. It's too stressful. I can't have Time Traveling Tina every other day making me crazy."

He stands to get off the bus and puts his hand on his hip as we arrive at his stop. He has to work tonight, or he'd come home with me like usual. "But, Dessy, since you're starting over, wear your other jeans. They make your butt look better. Also, wear that yellow tank you have with your jean jacket over it. And please go back in time as soon as you get home so I can skip work tonight and not have to do it twice."

"I can try to wear a different outfit before I go back, but I don't think it works that way. I think I'll be in the same clothes I was the first time around. As for work, you wouldn't remember it anyway." I laugh at how serious he looks right now, but I know it's crazy.

"Damn," he says, looking up and down at what I'm wearing now. "Well, my body would remember if I worked and I'm already tired. Dang."

"I'll see you back here in like twenty minutes, but it'll be 7:15 AM again. I can't believe you don't like what I'm wearing. I thought I looked cute."

"Sure, okay." He shakes his head and turns to go. "Bye, Shannon," he says as he gets off the bus.

"Later, man," Shannon says and gives him the peace sign.

While I wait to get to my house, I replay my conversation with Frankie from this morning, again trying to think of ways I can make it seem more natural but with more feeling if that's even possible. Rafa's right, this is an opportunity to step up my game. I'm just not sure how without it seeming forced. We didn't have to force anything before.

Pulling up to the house, I see Justine and her clunker parked in my driveway. She's talking to my brother and with every step she takes closer to him, he steps back. He looks to be arguing with her.

My body stiffens. He's trying to walk away from her, but she's grabbing his arm and pleading with him. It's shocking to see him treat her this way. This is very very bad. Is she that crazy over him that she came over here to tell him what I said today without even giving me the chance to talk to him like I said I would? He probably thinks she's gone mad if she's telling him I said he loves her.

Shannon stops the bus, watching the drama on my driveway. She gives a long, slow whistle. "Somebody's pissed off, man."

I dash off the bus and run as fast as I can past Jojo and Justine, barely even looking at them as I head to the backyard.

The last thing I hear is Jojo yelling for me.

Chapter Twenty-Five

Back on the bus, after furiously swinging back, my head is dizzy, and my body has that weird off kilter feeling I get after going back. I waste no time sitting down beside Rafa and yanking his notebook free from his stack of books and papers to show him where we signed it just minutes ago.

"Damn. The writing is gone." I say, scanning the notebook frantically.

"Writing? What writing?"

"We both signed and dated right here." I point to the blank spot. "So you would know when I've gone back in time and when we are doing this all over again."

"You better not be playing with me." He runs his hands over his face and looks around.

I take a deep breath and explain it all over to him again—about Justine and the bathroom and all the drama. "This is so wacky. I don't feel any different even though you're messing with my life." He looks down and rubs his arms up and down with both hands and then touches his hair.

I nod. "Sorry about that, but I didn't figure you'd know that I went back in time even with me telling you that we have to redo this day. And stop fidgeting, we are fine. You still look the exact same as the last time we did this."

"It's like any other Monday morning. That's good I guess." He shakes it off, and I hand him my brush and ponytail holder.

"Can you make it looser than you did before? It gave me a headache."

He lets out a tsk and turns me around so he can get started. I fill him in on what already happened with

Mr. Tim and how I need to catch Frankie this morning … again.

"Couldn't you have worn your other jeans. I don't like these as much."

"Rafa?"

"Mmhmm?"

"You literally said that to me about forty-five minutes ago, before I went back."

He finds this hilarious. "Well, at least I'm consistent in my advice, no matter when I give it."

"True," I say, with anxiety running through my whole body at the thought of seeing Frankie and getting to talk to him. I have a few ideas for conveying my emotions toward him without making him aware of my intentions.

The bus pulls up to the school, and this time I know exactly what bus Frankie's on. I stand before the bus stops, and Shannon yells, "Down in the back, man! It's not safe to stand before I stop."

"Girl, sit down. You know Shannon don't play about bus rules." Rafa pulls me down next to him. "Calm down. You know what bus he's on. You'll find him."

As much as a free spirit Shannon seems to be, she doesn't like us breaking safety rules. She takes her job seriously, and I can't fault her for that even if she probably goes home and smokes a pile of marijuana after work. Oddly, she's not wearing the same striped overalls, and now that I look at Rafa, he's dressed differently too. I wonder why things like clothes changed for them but not me. This is new. Before I swung away almost four years, clothes and things stayed the same when I swung away a bad moment. I'm curious about that but don't have time to keep pondering it.

Waiting for Shannon's slow butt to make a full stop, I stand slightly so I can scan the crowd for Frankie.

I wish Rafa would've picked a seat closer to the front of the bus since he gets on before me, but he wouldn't have known to do that, and we always sit in the same seat near the middle.

"I don't see Frankie." Panic rises in my throat, and I cough it back. If I don't find him and talk to him, then our time together the first time around never happened.

"Was he already off the bus by now the first time?"

"I think so. Last time, I hurdled myself over all the bus seats to get out there."

"Then get going!" This time he grabs all my books from me and yells, "Go, go, go."

I don't have such an easy time clearing the seats so seamlessly like before. Before I did it without thinking. This time I am thinking too much, and my legs aren't gliding over the seatbacks.

Stumbling onto the front sidewalk, I search the crowd. I look back and see that Frankie's bus is almost empty. After a minute of searching, Rafa comes to stand beside me as I whip my head in all directions.

He looks around with me. Suddenly, he loudly sucks in a breath as if he just saw a cheetah running across the school lawn. He grabs his chest with his free hand. "Oh, hell," he says, apprehensively handing me my books back, distracting me from something.

"What? What? Oh, hell what?" And then I see what he sees.

Frankie's standing at the front door, lovingly holding the hand of an unfamiliar petite black-haired girl. It's definitely not Aubrey. The girl sort of looks like me from this distance. I narrow my eyes and tilt my head, attempting to catch a glimpse of her face and confirm he's actually holding her hand. I run toward them before

Rafa knows what I'm doing.

"No! Dessy, Des. Stop!"

Rafa knows I'm about to lose it and probably humiliate myself.

By the time I catch up to him, he's holding the door open for everyone and the girl's inside patiently waiting for him. Does this guy ever not hold the door for people? Kids are just walking past, not even thanking him, lost in their own teen angst. I know him well enough to know he doesn't care. He doesn't expect a thank you.

I come to a halt in front of him, panting, and gaze deeply into his eyes. The whites of his eyes are pure and bright like him, accentuating the richness of the blue. I take in his perfect black eyebrows delicate but thick framing them. My eyes travel down to his mouth with his lips slightly parted, showing his two adorable, crooked teeth on the bottom.

He smiles at me, and I know it's a smile of hesitation and uncertainty as to why I'm directly in front of him, staring at him so intently, unable to catch my breath. In his mind, the last time I saw him was at Pete's when I tried buying him and Aubrey dinner. I never even said goodbye I was such a mess.

"Hi."

That's all I can think to say. I just want a moment like the first time we locked eyes on each other at Dax's BBQ. I just want a connection with him. Something, anything to know that we're soulmates.

"Hey." He's still holding the door as kids are rushing past us.

Rafa comes up beside me. "Hey, Frankie. Aren't you Mr. Door Holder Dan this morning?"

Frankie laughs as Rafa breaks the strange moment we were having and tries normalizing the situation.

"Yeah, well, I sort of got stuck. Nobody took over

the job," he says, chuckling, but he's still looking at me.

"We got you," Rafa says and moves to stand beside Frankie and take over the door.

"Thanks, I appreciate it. See you guys later." As Frankie turns and goes into the school, the girl who was waiting on him—looking so much like me it's freaky—holds out her hand. He leans in, taking it and kissing her cheek. I just about collapse right then and there. Blood surges through me, and I can hear my heartbeat in my ears.

Rafa grabs my hand.

I immediately shake it off and the tears start coming. "Rafa, I'm sorry, but I'm going back again. Something is off. I'm going back to 7:15 AM today ... again.

Before he can object, I break into a sprint toward my house, fueled by the rush of adrenaline coursing through me. I'm grateful I live so close to the school, even though I could probably run a marathon with the energy I possess at the moment. The events that just unfolded with Frankie and whoever that girl was didn't happen before, so why was it different this time? I can't get the image of him kissing her out of my head. I want to throw up.

When I get onto my street, I see my mom sitting outside on her porch swing reading, and I assume waiting for my dad to finish his morning poop. My parents' routine is like clockwork in the morning before they go into the shop.

As soon as she catches sight of me, I come to a quick halt in the middle of the street.

She stands up, her forehead furrowed in concentration. I can see the distinct vertical line forming between her eyebrows from where I stand. "Dessy? What are you doing home? What's wrong?"

Thinking as quick as I can and hoping the run dried up all my tears, I say, "I forgot my algebra homework, and it counts as a huge part of my grade. I left it on my bed with my folder." I speed walk to her. I need to just get to the swing, but I know I have to deal with this first.

"You could've called us. We would've brought it to you." She grabs hold of my shoulder and then pats my back. "Go in and get it. We can drive you back to school. I'm glad to see you taking so much initiative with your algebra grade. I know you hate it."

While she smiles, there's an underlying sense of profound wonder emanating from her expression. She's no dummy—her intuition is telling her something is not quite right. Her mom gut is kicking in, and her instincts are warning her there's an issue here, but she doesn't know what.

My dad comes waltzing out with the newspaper and the lunch bags he packed for them. "Des, what are you doing home?" He pushes his glasses up the bridge of his nose to get a better look at me.

"She forgot her algebra. We're going to take her back to school."

"Algebra's awful. I'd forget it too."

Mom pokes him in the side. "Hurry up, we gotta get to the shop. We'll wait in the car," my mom says as they saunter down the driveway.

"Okay, I'm hurrying," I say, as I run in the house. After closing the door behind me, I pivot to glance out of the small window next to the front door. I patiently wait for both of them to get in the car.

My dad's fiddling with one of my mom's lavender bushes, the one that's on its last leg and I know will die. He plucks off a leaf and scrutinizes it, despite having zero knowledge about gardening.

My mom gestures for him to get in the car and leave her bush alone. If either of them had a clue about bushes, they'd see that the downspout overwatering it is killing it.

As soon as he turns to get in the car, I race through the kitchen and out the backdoor. Hurling myself into the swing seat, I quickly glance to see if I'm alone.

Here we go again.

CARRIE BEAMER

Chapter Twenty-Six

I step on the bus and my mind jolts to attention like my body was just doused in ice water. Shannon's not in the driver's seat. Instead, an elderly man sporting a high and tight haircut, who I bet to be retired from the military, gives me a disapproving look and instructs me to hurry up. Wondering if I mistakenly got on the wrong bus, I realize it can't be the case as the bus stopped in front of my house and I'm the only passenger at my stop. I search the bus for Rafa and relax a little when I see that at least he's sitting in our normal seat.

"Stop dawdling and take your seat," the man barks at me.

I rush toward Rafa and plop down.

"Girl, why are you moving so slow? You know Jim doesn't play. He keeps a strict schedule down to the second."

I don't even answer his questions I'm so freaked out. "Rafa, who is Jim? Where the hell is Shannon?"

"Shannon? I don't know a Shannon." He looks around.

"Shannon has always been our bus driver. You know the large hippie gal who sports a bandana who we all sort of love in a weird bus driver way? I've never met Jim. Jim has never driven this bus. Is he a sub?"

"Jim has always been the bus driver. We don't know a Shannon."

"Rafa, I swung back again. We are doing this whole bus ride again, but Shannon who has always been our bus driver was here last time, not whoever Jim is."

"Again, why are we doing this again? What is going on that you keep taking us back? Is it a Frankie thing?"

I start sweating. Did I erase Shannon from the universe, or is she driving a different bus and somehow it all got switched? "This is not good, Raf. You don't remember, but our bus driver is not Jim. I've somehow altered things and now we have Jim. Jim sucks, by the way. And Frankie has a girlfriend that mysteriously looks like me … or at least he did. It's why I went back again, so I can see if it changes things … again."

Opening and then closing his mouth, he pauses. His lip looks like it's quivering for a second and his eyes fill. This is a lot to take in. He's shaking his head and looking at the other kids. I think he's checking to see if any of the kids on the bus are different, which has me doing the same thing. From what I can tell, everyone is still here. Rafa wouldn't know if anything is different, but he's inspecting everyone as if he would.

Elliot and Misty are still sitting across from us, drawing their comics and eating Skor candy bars for breakfast like usual. Carrie and Justin are still enthralled with each other in the seat diagonal from us. I don't think they ever stop kissing. I pop up quickly and peek to see if Bobby and Billy, the Callahan twins that I can never tell apart, are sitting in front of us. It's a relief to see their familiar, wavy red-haired heads.

"Hey, sit down," Jim yells from his pedestal of control up front. Bus drivers really hate when you stand while the bus is moving for some reason.

I flip him the bird but behind my seat of course. It makes me feel better. The middle finger is my go-to when I need to tell someone off in secret. I stick my middle finger up in the air almost every morning at my brother's adjoining wall when his clock radio wakes me up. God forbid he turn it down to a normal level and have some respect for the rest of the house. I really forgot what a total self-absorbed ass he was before, and now I have that self-absorbed ass back.

"I think we're good. Nothing else seems to have changed." I give his hand a quick squeeze to calm him.

He looks even more stressed and starts fanning himself with his notebook.

"Are you okay? You look like you might get sick."

He drops his notebook on his lap. "What if you altered my situation? What if my Aunt Kristi isn't set to land on Thursday to get all this paperwork going to take me to California? I will die. I can't go back to having no family. I just can't. What do we do?"

"Let's calm down for a sec. I don't think I've messed up your situation, because I've never met Kristi. That wouldn't change. I don't know her yet, and she's not played a role in anything with my going back right now. Shannon was here."

Although there isn't any consistency in anything I've noticed with time travel. Thank God that who I tell I can time travel remembers that part. Convincing Rafa I can time travel over and over would suck.

He sits back in his seat and nods. "You're probably right. But, Des, this has to stop. No more going back. You're keeping me from seeing my aunt even if I don't feel stuck. Plus, who knows where the hell Shannon went."

"You're right, I know you're right. This is going to make me crazy trying to change and fix everything. I'm gonna check all the buses for Shannon, or I'll never sleep tonight."

Now I'm fanning myself with his notebook.

"Whatever happens today you're going to roll with it no matter how bad it is. Do you hear me? Promise me." He holds out his pinkie finger for a pinky promise.

"What's this? We don't do pinky promises."

"We don't? Oh, hell. Okay then." He puts his hand down.

Did we used to pinky promise in his memory, I wonder. Is this another odd change like the school schedules? This is all getting to be too much.

"I promise Raf, I'm done going back."

"Good. Now turn around so I can do something with that hair. Why does it look like you haven't even combed it?"

"You try time traveling and see how you look. I'm a complete mess."

"You can say that again, sheesh."

This time I don't look for Frankie. I'm exhausted, and I'm afraid of what I'll find. Instead, I'm going to class to think. Shannon's disappearance and the bus ride has me rattled. Before we part ways for first hour, I tell Rafa he needs to take a sick day from work today and join me for some indulgent burger and onion rings therapy at Pete's after school, especially since he's going to move away soon and won't even need the job.

Rafa readily agrees without much persuasion, saying Mondays are slow at the record store and they will be okay without him. I just hope my first hour didn't change again. I guess I'll see.

****

I'm so over my algebra class. I can't believe I have to struggle through this again. Walking to second hour, I pass Jojo and some girl. He has his arm draped around her shoulders. Maybe that's Marianne Fremont because it's not Justine or Samantha. I tell myself I'm not getting involved. If I've learned anything in the past twenty-four hours, it's that I can't meddle in his relationship issues. I came back here to do one thing and that was give him football back even if that turned him into a cheating jerk. Rafa's with me on this journey, and he's right. It's time I listened to his much-needed, sound advice.

"Hey, Jo."

"Hey, Des."

As we pass each other, I overhear him speak to the girl in a playful discreet murmur. "That's my younger sister Dessy. She's a real pain in the ass."

As they walk away, she glances back at me and winks while popping a bubble with her gum. Who in the hell does that?

I can't believe he has the balls to call me a pain in the ass. I gave up everything for him. My brother is a major asshole.

****

After the longest day of my life, the final bell rings. I haven't run into Frankie one time and while I'm upset about that, I'm trying to let today pass calmly so I can at least get to tomorrow. I meet Rafa at our locker. "Hey, I'm going to run and check all the buses real fast to find Shannon."

"Well, don't be late. Trust me, Jim will leave your butt behind."

"Can we just walk to my house? We've been on that bus so much—I need a break."

In Rafa's mind we've been on the bus once, but I feel like all I've done is ride that dang thing.

"That's fine. Meet me by the crosswalk after you find Shannon. Please God find her."

"Got it." I walk as fast as I can without looking out of place to the first bus in the bus line. No Shannon. I move on to the second bus, then the third. When I get to the fourth bus, I hear her voice.

"Hey, man, you can't draw on the seats. That's not cool, man."

I release a huge breath and burst into happy laughter. I peek inside and there's Shannon in a bright yellow corduroy jumpsuit with a matching headband. "Hi, Shannon."

Shannon looks down at me and I can tell she has no idea who I am, but she still says, "Hey, man, how's it going?"

Seeing her is everything right now. I'd love to go up and give her a high five, but I feel it'd be a strange thing to do. I settle for a friendly farewell. "Bye, Shannon."

"Later, man," she says, turning back to the hoodlums behind her that were drawing on her seat.

I didn't erase her after all. Rafa's going to be elated, because he still looked terrified that I could've erased his Aunt Kristi when I saw him at our lockers. I pivot to exit the bus doorway and give way to let the actual riders of this bus board.

"Hi, Dessy," Frankie says from behind me.

Has he been standing behind me this whole time waiting to get on his bus? I didn't even think about the fact that this could be his bus with how jumbled up things have gotten. And I'm not wearing the dang jeans Rafa says make my butt look cute. Ugh.

I snap out of it. "Hey, Frankie."

He steps back to let another kid pass him to get on the bus.

"Isn't Shannon the best?" He gestures toward her, and she gives us both the peace sign and a wide grin displaying a set of silver teeth that look pretty bad ass. I never noticed her teeth before, which is out of character for me—I love funky teeth. We all have our things.

"So, what happened at Pete's the other night? I looked for you after we got our food, but you sort of disappeared."

"Oh, yeah. I, um … had to get home. My brother came to Pete's and said my mom needed me. Sorry I didn't say bye. I was kind of in a rush. When moms need help, it's not up for debate."

My heart's beating so fast that my blood feels like it's pumping through my body in overdrive, making my arms feel heavy. I'm proud of myself for responding to his question with a believable and somewhat normal answer.

"Boy, do I get that. Well, maybe we can hang out there again sometime." And with that, he steps on the bus. "See you later."

"See ya."

I turn to walk away as cool as I can with my jaw dropped and my stomach doing flip flops. I make it to Rafa and I can hardly contain my happiness.

"What took you so long? Please tell me that smile means you found Shannon?"

CARRIE BEAMER

Chapter Twenty-Seven

"Rafa! Holy crap! I saw him and he spoke to me! It wasn't weird. It was natural and normal and wonderful. Oh, and yes, I found Shannon. She's Frankie's bus driver now. Can you believe that?"

He slaps his forehead with the palm of his hand, flabbergasted.

We walk all the way to Pete's without even stopping in at my house. Rafa thinks it is best for me mentally to avoid whatever the hell Jojo could be doing at the house with any number of girls. Him craving the onion rings I promised probably has something to do with us not stopping as well. Thanks to my meltdown, he got screwed out of his onion rings last time.

On our walk I take him through the whole scenario blow by blow. I explain how I only stopped in the bus doorway because I couldn't help but to say hello to Shannon after mixing her life up in the last day.

"So, what you're saying is the great bus driver swap of the 80s worked in your favor?"

We both stop walking as it hits us both at once.

"Do you think the universe put Shannon on Frankie's bus so I'd go looking for her and bump into him? Could that really be why it happened?"

"I think we're stuck with Jim is what I think."

He's downplaying the whole scenario because I know this stuff creeps him out.

"But really, Raf. Is this possible?"

"How in the Baffled Bob would I know? Don't start thinking that going back is the answer to your problems because of this. The reason you spoke with Frankie without making it happen is because you're finally listening to me. You let it just happen after going through a normal day."

We start walking again.

"True. I wish I could've had more time to think of a response when he said we should hang out again sometime though."

"You don't need more time to have that mouth of yours get you in trouble. You need to take it slow. The good news is that means he's interested, so maybe that Dessy clone you saw him with isn't around anymore. Maybe she got altered into being one of Jojo's new girls."

"Rafa!"

He lets out the loudest cackle. "You gotta admit I'm funny as hell."

"Not funny." I can't help but laugh too. "I'd rather her be with Jojo than Frankie, but since she looks like me that would be yucky if my brother was dating her."

"Ew, that is nasty."

This makes us both crack up. It's so good to laugh. Laughing with your best friend has to be the best medicine for a bad day. Especially when you redid that day twice.

We get to Pete's before anyone else is there. It's early and even Jake the Gigolo hasn't arrived to work the dinner shift yet, which is nice. He makes ordering food a very unpleasant experience for me.

Rafa gets two orders of onion rings and a large Dr. Pepper. "Don't judge me. I'm about to move to California, and I'm not sure I'll find these same onion rings out there. My plan is to load up while I can."

"No judgement here. This has been a day," I say as I order two cheeseburgers with extra pickles and a large Dr. Pepper of my own.

In this moment, I understand how resorting to food as a source of comfort during difficult times may feel like the only way to find solace and happiness. My mind goes to Jojo and how food was everything to him. He found happiness in Justine when he was stuck in his room, but I think food was what brought him the comfort he needed just to find something to look forward to every day.

We slide into a booth, and I stare at my cheeseburgers. Sadness washes over me. I don't know how I could've changed any of that for Jojo. As I gaze over at the booth that Frankie and I used to call our own, I can't help but feel a sense of sorrow for everything that has been lost. Pete's brings it all back, and there's nothing I can do about any of it.

My thoughts are interrupted by Jake.

He slides in next to me. "Hey, babe."

Jake leans in and kisses my cheek, and I'm too stunned to stop it from happening.

"Babe? Get out of here!" I shove him so hard he falls out of the booth and onto the floor.

Rafa drops the onion ring he was getting ready to take a bite of and stands up. "Boy, have you lost your mind?" Rafa's so mad I can see the vein in his neck pulsing. He points a finger still covered in onion ring grease at Jake. "You don't go kissing people that don't want to be kissed. I swear I should…"

Jake interrupts him from the floor. "What do you mean? I kiss her every day after school. What's wrong with you guys?"

The look on Jake's face is one of pure shock. He's not putting on his usual act. His face is purely genuine.

"You think we're together?" I say in disbelief.

"Think? Dessy, we've been together since summer. Why are you being this way?"

"Oh shit," Rafa blurts out. "I'm getting a weird like deja vu thing happening, Des. I think you *are* dating him, but I had a sudden gut instinct telling me otherwise. How did I not remember about your boyfriend? Why did I suddenly feel like you can't stand him? What the hell is happening to me?"

"Maybe it's because I told you." I look at Jake, very aware he is hanging onto our every word. "Well, you know I told you my special thing. Maybe you can get glimpses of things that have happened even though you had no clue who Shannon was. Oh man this is getting bizarre."

Rafa and I look at each other over the table, trying to make sense of it all.

"What are you guys talking about?" Jake asks from the floor.

"Jake, my man, the universe is definitely not working in your favor," Rafa says. He extends his hand to help Jake up. Rafa has quickly accepted the fact that Jake's life has been changed, and even though he sucks, this one isn't his fault.

"Jake, we're going need you to go over there for a minute." Rafa points over to me and Frankie's booth.

"But—" Jake tries to protest while he wipes the floor grime from his work pants.

"No buts. Get over there and get over there right now. Move it!" Rafa says it so firmly that Jake briefly looks from me and back to him before quickly walking away. He doesn't go sit in the booth. He goes behind the counter and to the back room.

"Oh my God!" I start pacing the back of the restaurant. Thankfully nobody is back here.

"Now listen to me, Des. I know you think you need to go back, but what if it's worse the second time around? And now you've got me remembering things I never knew about. I'm trying not to think about what that can mean. Maybe nothing. Hell, I don't know!"

"I can't believe this. How can this be happening? This can't be real. I would never date him!"

Rafa starts manically eating his onion rings. "I'm stressed. Stop looking at me. I'm trying to process."

"Can we just get out of here, please? I can't be here right now. Pack up your onion rings. We gotta go."

Without any delay, he crams all his onion rings back into their container, even leaving one in his mouth to ensure he doesn't lose any of them again.

On the walk to my house, we run through how to handle this new development while Rafa devours his onion rings.

"This isn't the worst thing that could have happened. Keep the good things at the front of your mind. You were able to have a moment with Frankie today, and that could grow into something more. We feel good about that, remember?"

"I'm dating Jake!"

"Just go home, call Pete's, and dump him. You don't need time travel to dump an annoying guy."

He makes it seem so easy.

"I feel gross, like I need a shower. How could I be dating such a sleaze ball?"

"I mean you didn't really date him. It's been one day. Shoot, not even. It's been like twenty minutes."

"I know, but there has to be a version of me somewhere that's dating Jake. Right?"

"Now this is the type of thing that freaks me out. We can't go there. Let's concentrate on right now. I don't want to think about other Dessys—or Rafas for that matter. Just stop that."

We walk in silence for a bit before Rafa begins singing, bringing us both the ability to think calmly.

"Have you sung for your Aunt Kristi yet?"

He smiles wide. "Not yet."

"She's going to be blown away."

He sings all the way back to my street. Singing is Rafa's comfort.

I know I can't keep going back. What if I did mess up this whole thing with his aunt or even alter it somehow? I can't risk that. Rafa doesn't deserve it. I have to handle life the way it is. Jojo's playing football, Rafa's leaving foster care, and I have something I can maybe get going with Frankie.

When we get to my house, Justine is sitting on the hood of her car. She's crying, and Jojo's truck is not even here.

"Stay out of it, Des. You promised you wouldn't go back. Get in there, call and dump Jake, then take a shower and do your homework. Let everything else go. You promised." He holds up his pinkie finger for a pinky promise.

"I told you we don't do pinky promises."

He holds his pinkie up in my face. "We do now."

I lock pinkies with him and look him dead in the eye. "I promise."

Chapter Twenty-Eight

Justine trails behind me into the house like we're old friends, and now I wonder if we are. At this point, anything's possible I suppose.

She scoops up Pony and gives him a cuddle. She always did love that evil fluff ball. "I've been waiting to talk to you, but your bus just blew past the house."

"Talk to me about what?" I'm trying to gage what she knows and where her head is at. I have no idea when she thinks we last spoke—I can't keep track of it all. I need her to go away so I can call Pete's and break up with Jake.

"About Jojo?" She follows me in the kitchen and hops up to sit on the counter just like she always used to do.

"What about Jojo?" I grab a Jell-O pudding pop from the freezer, trying to get more information out of her. I have no idea how to respond.

The thunderous roar of Jojo's truck fills the room, warning of us of his arrival.

With a sense of urgency, she swiftly leaps off the counter and frantically snatches her purse and shoes. "I have to get out of here," she says, going for the back door instead of the front.

"He knows you're here. Your car is in the driveway. Why are you running away?"

The front door slams open with a resounding crash, causing us to jolt in surprise. Jojo charges in like a fierce bull stampeding toward his target. I wonder if I'll ever grow used to the reality of his renewed vigor and good health. It catches me off guard each time I see it.

"Justine, what the hell are you doing here? I told you to leave me alone. Can you not get that through your thick head?"

With her hand resting on the back door, she suddenly becomes motionless, freezing in place. She looks down, fixated on some unseen object, as her shoulders start heaving up and down with deep, sorrowful sobs.

"Here we go again with the waterworks. I'm over it. The pity party needs to stop."

"Hey! Don't you dare speak to her that way!" I'm yelling as I cross the kitchen and meet him where he's standing. "Who the hell do you think you are?" I rise up onto my tiptoes, straining to meet his gaze directly at eye-level.

He looks away from me and back over to Justine. "Mind your own business, Dessy." He shouts at me, but he's still looking at Justine.

"This is my business. I gave you football back. I lost everything for you! Who are you? This isn't the Jojo I know. You love her."

With my pudding pop in hand, I gesture toward Justine. She remains stationary, her hand resting on the back door, seemingly at a loss for words or actions. This reaction appears to still be her default mode when confronted with uncertainty or confrontation.

"I love her? Uh, no. I broke up with her and she keeps coming back like a lost dog."

I hurl my pudding pop across the room in anger, and I hear a thud from behind Jojo. I look around him to find my mother standing there with her purse on the ground, her face frozen in a bewildered expression. We didn't even hear her come in.

"Dessy, I need to see you outside please." She speaks in such a calm voice it scares me. My mom isn't the one that usually stays calm in tense situations.

"See me outside? I didn't do anything. Jojo's in

here treating Justine like dirt and—"

She interrupts me. "Now, Dessy. Let's go."

My dad walks in with a sprig of lavender bush leaf clutched in his hand. He knows something's going down. The mood in this house is so tense that taking a deep breath feels like a challenge.

"Joseph, I need you to stay in here and calm things down while I go talk to Dessy."

He stops inspecting the leaf in his hand and nods. Sitting down on the living room couch, ready to listen to whoever might need him right now, he takes his glasses off and sets them on the coffee table.

I remain rooted in place for what feels like a full minute, challenging her ask of me with my eyes.

Finally, she extends her hand toward me.

Not even Jojo has moved. He knows our mom heard him acting awful. Like me, I think he's wondering why I'm being taken outside for a talk and not him.

"This is ridiculous, Mom. I'm defending Justine, and now I'm in trouble? For what?"

She ignores me and grabs my arm, practically pulling me out of the house. She guides me to the porch swing by placing her hands on my shoulders and gently but firmly directing me to sit down.

"Mom, do you have any idea what's being going on with Jojo and Justine?"

She nods. "I know exactly what's going on."

I turn my gaze toward her.

She shuts her eyes tight and starts moving the swing back and forth using both her feet.

The rumble starts immediately.

CARRIE BEAMER

Chapter Twenty-Nine

As I stand at the entrance to Jojo's room, I watch Frankie counting down for him as he sits on the edge of his bed, doing leg lifts with ankle weights firmly fastened around his feet.

Jojo's sweating through his shirt and the look of concentration spread across his face is pure agony, but he's pushing through.

"Good job, Jo! You did even more reps today than yesterday." Frankie raises his hand for a high-five.

Jojo reciprocates, looking almost identical to his appearance during my senior year of high school, with the exception of a slightly leaner face, hinting at some weight loss.

My mom comes behind me and says, "Got a minute?"

Frankie's standing in my house right now, and I am so speechless I cannot even find words to say anything to him. All I can do is follow her.

She leads me out back to my swing set. Selecting my mode of time travel, she sinks into the seat I normally use and motions for me to sit on the other side.

She sighs deeply. "Well, Dessy, I was hoping you wouldn't make the discovery on your own, but it seems that was very unwise of me. Your Gran showed me this power when I turned seventeen, which is the age all women in our family gain their time travel wings. Your Gran's mom, Great Grandma Gillio, showed her the power at seventeen too, but with you, I wanted to wait. I didn't want you to know you had it for a long time. A seventeen-year-old can and will make a lot of damaging mistakes. I wanted you to find out when you were older. These mistakes can be a nightmare to deal with. I guess like mother like daughter." She laughs and reaches over to give my arm a squeeze.

"So, you knew? This whole time you knew what I was doing?" I'm not exactly welcoming her warm affection right now. I'm downright irritated.

"At first, it all seemed okay. You were doing what all the women in this family did when we learned of this power. You changed little details of your day here and there. I was proud that you didn't try using the power to get rich or anything like that. I knew once you realized the power you had that Jojo's situation would be a problem for you."

"And it wasn't for you?"

Why the hell didn't she fix my brother? She could've changed the situation the day it happened to him. A butterfly lands on the chain of my swing, and I wave it away. I'm angry and I don't want to see anything beautiful right now. Although, the sight of seeing my Frankie helping Jojo, and Jojo letting him, is the most beautiful thing I've seen in a long time.

"What happened to your brother was devastating, and I made a huge mistake trying to fix it. I did the one thing Gran told me to never do."

I twist my swing to face her.

"I told someone about my power." She closes her eyes in regret.

"Who did you tell?"

"I told your dad. He was so beside himself in the hospital the night your brother got hurt that I had to tell him. He's my best friend and my husband. I couldn't imagine making the choice to go back for Jojo without him knowing. I was scared and told him everything. That was a big no no. I knew I screwed up, but that night was devastating."

"So, you came home and got on your porch

swing? By the way, is it always a swing?"

She laughs. "It is always some type of swing. You could even use my porch swing or any swing you come across. Your Aunt Diana even used a swing at the state fair years ago to keep riding the same ride over and over until Gran got to her and stopped it. She would've ridden that big swing ride all weekend. Which brings me to another rule of this power, your elders can undo what you did."

I smile. I can picture my Aunt Diana doing this. She loves a good carnival. If there is a prize to be won at the fair, she wins it. Oh…Now I know why. She has intel.

"I knew there is rules I didn't know."

"I didn't know that one either for a long time. But yes, I came home and went back to the football play that hurt Jojo, but because I told your dad I was doing it, all hell broke loose. The play happened, but instead of Jojo getting hurt it was Dax Goulart. I had to keep undoing it until it was back to Jojo getting hurt. It was the biggest nightmare of my life, watching player after player get hurt. Unfortunately, Gran passed away last year—she couldn't fix what I was doing."

"Oh. My. God. I can't believe that. And to think I thought I'd been through hell. I can't imagine what you had to go through."

She clears the tears that have trickled down from her eyes. "Honestly, I was hoping you wouldn't discover your power for a long time, because it comes with a heavy burden when something goes wrong with someone you love."

"I told Rafa." I blurt my mistake out.

"Ah, I figured you told someone. You were so anxious to help Jojo that you didn't see what I saw coming. You went back to freshman year, all the while Jojo was here finally ready to change things for himself.

You were just missing it. I had to find you and undo what you were doing. I'll tell you how to do that someday. It can get very confusing. My tip off was that I had Jojo's football uniform in the dirty laundry, and he hasn't played in almost four years."

She winks at me, and now I'm crying.

"Jojo was going to get help, but he wasn't ready to be forced into it."

"I've tried so hard, Mom. All I wanted was for him to be healthy and happy."

She pulls a tissue out of her jacket pocket and hands it to me.

Now I'm the one doing the clarinet nose blowing.

"Dessy, I feel proud to be your mother when I see what you gave up for Jojo. I don't know very many people that would do something like that for another person. Your heart is always in the right place. But ... you can't choose people's lives for them. This power doesn't give us the right to alter someone's timing."

"I'm learning that the hard way." Both of us are laughing as tears stream down our faces.

"This power doesn't allow us to make someone fall in or out of love. We can't stop someone from dying, and we certainly can't choose how someone handles their own tragedy. It comes down to timing for each person. Timing is everything. It causes all the good things that will happen to someone and the bad, too. But it's their timing to experience and not for us to decide. Timing is a personal journey, and we can't alter it for someone else. We can use this power for ourselves, but not at the cost of a catastrophic change in someone's else's life. Relive a great day, but don't try to change that great day too much. That's the secret to this power. It's a gift once you know how to use it."

I stand up and go to her. She pulls me in for a

hug, and I wipe my face on her shirt just like I did when I was little. It feels so good. I feel safe for the first time in months. Every brick that has built a house on my chest is lifted, and I can see it all so clearly now.

"Relish the love you have and let timing do the rest." She kisses me on my forehead as I release her.

The creak of the patio screen door opening carries over to us.

"Hey, Des, are we still going to Pete's for a burger? If so, we better get going."

I turn to look behind me, and there's Frankie standing by the back door, looking just like the boy I went to senior prom with. The boy who taught me that helping others can look many different ways. The boy that I'm never going to let go of.

As I go to him and take his hand, I look into those blue eyes. And I know I'm finally where I'm supposed to be.

CARRIE BEAMER

Epilogue

"What's for dinner?" I ask, approaching Justine and Frankie, who have their heads pressed together over a book.

Whatever they're trying to figure out, it's causing them both to have furrowed brows. They're lost in deep concentration.

Browsing through Frankie's microbiology books, I know I could never be in nursing—I'll stick with journalism. With our significantly different majors, Frankie and I don't have any college classes together, but Justine has one class with him, and it warms my heart to see them study together.

She has been a big help to Frankie, being two years ahead of him. Her decision to apply to Southwest Missouri State and go to college with us has been life changing for her. She's graduating in a month and already has a nursing job secured in Nebraska. She's not going back home because there's not a lot to go home for. While she'll always remain near and dear to my family, it's important for her to prioritize her own desires and goals now. Justine deserves to build a life that brings her happiness, and that's exactly what she's doing.

"Hey." Frankie looks up and meets my smile with a kiss.

"I would really love to get a pizza. I'm craving the new taco pizza Godfather's Pizza has on promotion this month," Justine says, still looking down at the book.

"Oh, hell yes. I'm in. Every time I see the commercial playing in the resident hall, I practically drool." I laugh, but it's true. "You guys finish up. I'm gonna run to the apartment and change."

Justine and I share an apartment off campus. I'm

going to miss her so much next year. The apartment, with its bright yellow walls and oddly adorned pink flamingos painted all over them, rarely has working hot water or air conditioning, but it's saving us both a ton of money. Rafa says it sounds like the Ritz Carlton compared to some of the places he grew up living in. Waitressing on weekends allows us both enough money in tips to pay the rent.

Frankie lives in the dorms as a resident assistant. He gets free room and board, but I swear he'd do it even if he didn't receive compensation. He takes great pleasure in assisting the freshmen and being the go-to person they can rely on for help, no matter the time of day or night.

Once Jojo made up his mind to get healthy, Justine and Jojo realized what their relationship was. For Justine, it was someone to take care of. She had spent most of their relationship planning her entire life around taking care of him. She felt a responsibility to him, and he felt stuck. Stuck in his bad choices, stuck in his love for Justine—who was clearly unhappy— and stuck trying to figure out what to do next.

Judy Shewy helped them both understand that they had an unhealthy dependence on one another. Justine was afraid of abandonment. Latching on to someone who literally couldn't abandon her was something she didn't even realize she was doing. Jojo was afraid that losing Justine meant losing who he used to be. She was his last connection to the life he lost after he was hurt.

How I missed all of this is beyond me. I truly believed they were soulmates and that they couldn't possibly want to separate their lives. I viewed their feelings for each other as the same that Frankie and I felt. That's where I went wrong. Viewing everyone from my own lens.

I looked Judy up after my mom brought me back

to present day. Of course, she didn't remember ever meeting me or being in my house the first time, but she knew exactly what was going on with Justine and Jojo— she did her homework. I didn't call her for my brother this time. I called her to help Justine.

My brother spent all his time working out and getting acclimated to being a part of the day-to-day life of our family again. He began cooking the family meals. At first, he needed a large stool at the stove, but as he got stronger, he was able to stand and maneuver the whole kitchen. After the first year of his weight loss journey, he began taking long, slow walks alone. I think he was rebuilding himself on those walks, mentally and physically My parents began a workout program with him. Justine seemed like the lost dog Jojo accused her of being during my brief time back in 1981. That jerky Jojo never reappeared, thank God.

I thought Justine needed someone to help her out of the rut she was in. I was only going to try once—no more forcing my ideas on anyone. I told myself if it went badly with Justine and Judy, I wasn't going to swing it away. I was going to let it go. Turns out, Judy was precisely what Justine needed, even though Jojo thought Judy was a bit of a strange bird. Judy's the whole reason Justine ended up coming to college with me and Frankie. I love that crazy hula hoop lady. Justine still calls her once a week to get advice.

I've learned to embrace bad days, to accept them and move on to the next. Taking my mom's advice, I only swing back now to relive a really great moment. Trying to make happiness for myself or someone I love isn't ever going to work when it isn't happening naturally.

My mom erased Rafa's knowledge of my time travel abilities when she overrode my trip back to our freshman year. I wish I could tell him and Frankie. It's strange to keep something so major from either one of them. My mom regularly reminds me of the mess it can cause. I get it, but it can be torture.

Frankie and I are spending the summer with Rafa in Los Angeles. His aunt lives in a house that Rafa does call the Ritz-Carlton—he's thriving. He attends Julliard School for musical art in New York during the year. I just know he's going to be a superstar. His aunt says she wants to spoil us this summer, and we wholeheartedly can't agree with her plan more.

As for Jojo, he's enrolled in the local community college. He's working toward being a dietician for hospitals with patients confined to their beds because of injury or illness. I don't think there are words to describe how proud I am of my brother. Over the past two years, he has faced the most challenging days of his life. But now, when my brother firmly sets his mind to something, he fearlessly works for it with unwavering resolve. I should've known he'd eventually get to this point, but my love and worry got in the way. Jojo would say it was my love and control.

I guess I can't argue with that. All I can do is change—without traveling back in time.

The End

Evernight Teen ®

www.evernightteen.com